rachel ward

BONNEVILLE
BOOKS

An Imprint of Cedar Fort, Inc.
Springville, Utah

ISBN 13: 978-1-4621-2101-4

Published by Bonneville Books, an imprint of Cedar Fort, Inc.
2373 W. 700 S., Springville, UT 84663
Distributed by Cedar Fort, Inc., www.cedarfort.com

LIBRARY OF CONGRESS CATALOGING-IN-PUBLICATION DATA

Names: Ward, Rachel, 1982- author.
Title: Right next to me / Rachel Ward.
Description: Springville, Utah : Bonneville Books, an imprint of Cedar Fort, Inc., [2017]
Identifiers: LCCN 2017017949 (print) | LCCN 2017023732 (ebook) | ISBN 9781462128396 (epub and moby) | ISBN 9781462121014 (perfect bound : alk. paper)
Subjects: | GSAFD: Love stories.
Classification: LCC PS3623.A7344 (ebook) | LCC PS3623.A7344 R54 2017 (print) | DDC 813/.6--dc23
LC record available at https://lccn.loc.gov/2017017949

Cover design by Priscilla Chaves
Cover design © 2017 by Cedar Fort, Inc.
Edited and typeset by Hali Bird and Jessica Romrell

Printed in the United States of America

10 9 8 7 6 5 4 3 2 1

Printed on acid-free paper

To Heather, without whom this book would not exist

OTHER BOOKS BY RACHEL WARD

Dear Jane

chapter one

I kind of always assumed that graduation would be this big, amazing event, liberating us from the tyranny of tardy bells, class schedules, and sadistic cliques. In truth, it was a little boring. I mean, there's a moment there where they call your name and you go up onstage and for one moment it's all about you. But otherwise, meh.

However, there is little that you could do to get me to admit that out loud. My boyfriend, Gavin, was our class valedictorian, so he spoke at our ceremony. At the end of August he's on a plane to Connecticut and I won't be seeing him again until Christmas. But I am not thinking about that today. Today I am thinking about the party tonight and trying to focus on Gavin's speech about reaching for our dreams and changing the world. He did well. But then, he always does. That's why he is the valedictorian.

1

There is a moment at the end of the graduation ceremony where everyone is supposed to throw their caps. But the senior advisors told us not to. Several times. Per minute.

"If you lose your cap, you don't get it back."

"If you lose your cap, you lose your tassel."

"If you lose your cap, it won't be in any of your graduation pictures."

So, only about half of us threw our caps. It was very anticlimactic. And then after the ceremony, it took about half an hour to find everyone. Piper was closest. (Madison, Piper, Morris, Sydney). It seemed appropriate though, that we ended this together: Piper and I had been friends since first grade. We wandered toward the exit and spotted James easily, almost a head taller than the rest of the blue and white herd. Piper found her boyfriend, Sean, and ran to him, throwing her arms around him and laughing. As we approached the dais, Gavin appeared at my side.

"You did good, man," James praised as Gavin pulled me in.

"You did," I repeated from his embrace, my voice muffled by his gown.

"Thanks," Gavin kissed the top of my head, a few copper strands attaching themselves to his five o'clock shadow, and then pulled on my hand. "Let's get out of here." He navigated out of the doors and we stepped out into the sunlight, immediately surrounded by parents. I glanced around at the crowd. Moms were crying, kids were yelling, and there was a lot of hugging and photography.

"I see my mom," I exclaimed, pointing through the crowd. "And yours," I announced to James. "C'mon." I let go of Gavin's hand and grabbed James, dragging him through the crowd. "Mom!" I shouted over the din. Somehow she heard me and turned in my direction. She was beaming. My sister, Whitney, was next to her, tapping the program against her leg impatiently. I released James and threw my arms around Mom's neck.

"Congratulations," she said, hugging me tightly. "You did it." She pulled away and posed me under a nearby tree for a picture. "Whitney," she called, "come be in the picture." Whitney made a face and trudged over. She plastered a fake smile on her face and as soon as Mom's camera clicked she was gone again.

"James," my mom called. He stood between his parents, laughing at the empty diploma cover. He turned toward us when he heard his name. She waved him over. "Come take a picture with Sydney." He handed his diploma to his mom and was next to me in a matter of strides. He wrapped his arm around me and we smiled as the camera clicked. He wrapped the other arm around me and pulled me into him.

"How you feeling?" he asked softly.

"Weird," I laughed. He pulled back and nodded. For most of my high school career it had been the five of us. Gavin, Sean, James, me, and Piper. The group had evolved naturally during our freshman and sophomore years. Gavin and Sean had been close since junior high school. Then Gavin and I got together after freshman year. James had moved into my neighborhood the summer before sophomore year and clicked immediately with all of us. And Piper and Sean hooked up at the beginning of junior year. We were always together, at least in some combination. But starting in the fall, that would change.

We were all set to head our separate ways. Gavin would go to Yale in Connecticut; he was the pride of our high school and the only one to be accepted into an Ivy League school. Piper was headed to USC. None of us are entirely sure how she got in, but I have a theory that it had something to do with generous donations from her father. Sean had gotten a full scholarship to Utah State and would be moving to Logan. James was accepted to the University of Utah, and was planning on living at home since it was only minutes away from campus. And I was headed north to Boise State University in Idaho to study graphic design.

"Sydney!" Gavin yelled my name across the crowd. Sean and Piper were next to him. I turned and smiled at him and beckoned to them.

"Come take pictures," I called. James stepped behind me and Gavin positioned himself on my left side. Piper snuck in and wrapped her arm around my neck and Sean stood next to James.

"Smile," Mom called. James's mom had sidled up next to her as well, camera at the ready. I knew that we had the whole summer before us, but there was something so final about this moment that my breath caught momentarily in my chest. Everything was changing.

"You want a ride tonight?" Gavin asked me as we finished with the pictures. Sean and Piper had disappeared and James had returned to his family. Mom and Whitney were waiting to take me home. I nodded. "I'll text you in a bit." He bent down and kissed me quickly and then he was back with his family as well.

My eyes scanned the crowd apprehensively as we walked back to the car. Whitney shot me a look. "You know he's not here, Syd."

"I don't know what you're talking about," I lied quickly, shifting my eyes to my feet. I felt Mom's hand on my arm. "I'm fine," I snapped, pulling away slightly, immediately sorry. It wasn't her fault that my dad couldn't care less about us. He lived out of state and only showed up very occasionally. I had hoped that maybe my graduation would warrant a visit, but it was stupid to get my hopes up. Something as minor as my high school graduation apparently wasn't worth a plane ticket.

"Should we get dinner before your grad night?" Mom asked as she pulled the car into the long line to exit the lot. "From Scratch?"

"Of course," I agreed readily. Dinner out was a luxury and dinner at my favorite restaurant was even less common. You haven't had potato chips until they've been made fresh for you.

"We'll pick up Tyler, then, and go." My nine-year-old brother had begged to be excused from the torture that is sitting still for two hours. She glanced over at me and smiled. "You know, you're a pretty okay kid."

I smiled. "You're not a terrible mom," I replied. Whitney groaned from the back seat and Mom laughed.

"Love you too, Whitney," Mom smiled into the rearview mirror and we finally made it to the end of the parking lot and out into the street.

chapter two

MARCH 2014

Thanks for the ride," I called pushing the door shut. There was one week left until the school art show and I had stayed late after school every day this week trying to finish up my last piece. I had three pieces in the show: one sketch and two computer illustrations. The last one was proving more difficult in execution than in theory and I didn't have the right programs on my laptop at home, so it all had to be done on school computers. It was very inconvenient. I swung my backpack over my shoulder and let myself in through the garage. We had lived in this house as long as I could remember and the garage code had never changed. I dropped my bag in the mudroom and stepped into the usually cheery kitchen. I knew immediately something was wrong.

The counter was a mess. Dirty dishes were strewn across it from breakfast and it looked like dinner was half made and abandoned on the stove. My mom wasn't a neat freak, but she was a clean cook. She never started a new meal until the last one had been cleared. The sink

5

was piled high and the dishwasher was open, half cleared. "Mom?" I called nervously.

The living room was empty. Tyler's kindergarten worksheets were strewn across the coffee table and his shoes were underneath it. I couldn't hear anything. "Hello?" I called up the stairs. "Where is everybody?"

A door slammed and Mom appeared at the top of the stairs, disheveled. Her face was blotchy and her eyes were swollen. My stomach dropped. "Mom?" I asked quietly. "What's going on?"

She came down the stairs slowly, her jaw set. "It's been a bad day, Syd."

"What's going on?" I asked, growing more and more nervous. "Where is Tyler and Whit?"

"They are both in their rooms," her voice cracked slightly as she spoke. "Sydney, there's something that we need to talk about." She reached out to me but I took a step back.

"Are you sick?" I asked weakly. She shook her head. "Grandma?" She shook her head again.

"Come and sit down," she beckoned toward the couch.

I took another step away from her. "Mom, what is going on?" I repeated. She swallowed hard.

"Some things have happened today and, uh," her voice cracked again, more noticeably this time. She cleared her throat and started again. "Your dad is going to be moving out."

I took another step backward and ran into the kitchen table. "What?" I asked softly.

"We are separating, your dad and I." Her hands tightened into fists as she struggled to maintain her composure.

"Why?" I whispered.

She took a deep breath. "Your dad and I need some time apart. We seem to have different priorities and it has become apparent that they are irreconcilable."

I leaned on the table for support. "What did he do?"

She shook her head. "You don't need to worry about that. He is still your father and—"

I cut her off. "Mom, I'm not a little kid."

"No," she agreed. "You're not." She let out a sigh, allowing her shoulders to slump forward. "I can't talk about it right now, Sydney. I can't." She shuffled toward the couch and slid onto it. "I just need help right now, honey. Do you think you could finish up dinner?"

I nodded and moved mindlessly into the kitchen. A million thoughts swirled in my head. They were separating. Did that mean divorce? Of course it did. I put the pot of pasta on the counter and hoped that it wasn't too soggy. Divorce. So, every other weekend? What would a weekend with just Dad be like? He was never around. He worked long hours and then traveled half of the time. Maybe divorce wouldn't be all that different. I pulled the spaghetti sauce out of the fridge. But this would mean that Mom would have to get a job. It wouldn't be that big of a deal, we were all in school now anyway, but what would she do? I knew that she had graduated from college but I couldn't remember her ever having a job.

I set plates on the kitchen table, and out of habit set a place for Dad. I pulled the pot off the counter and set it on the table, and as I turned around I realized what I had done. Dad would not be home for dinner tonight. I stared at his place for a moment, frozen by grief. He wasn't coming back. Life from here on out would be completely different. I swallowed a sob.

"Mom," I called, clearing the pain from my throat. "It's done."

The next week was one of the hardest of my life. I woke up, helped Tyler get some breakfast, and Whitney walked him to kindergarten. I went to school like I had every other day of my life. I stared blankly at the board in every class, barely hearing anything that was being said. I came home and made dinner. Mom had kind of checked out. She spent most of the day in her room, either zoned out with the TV on or sleeping. Whitney had stopped talking to everyone and instead stomped and slammed around the house. And I still didn't know what was coming. Most of Dad's stuff was still in his closet. But we didn't hear from him all week. I got a ride to the art show with my friend Beth's mom and

stood alone for most of the night. At the end of the evening Piper showed up with Sean and Gavin in tow.

"Hey," Piper hugged me quickly. She was the only one who knew what was going on. I could only handle saying it out loud once.

"Hi," I replied.

"They look really good," she said as she pointed to the three framed pieces behind me with a smile. "I really like them."

"Thanks."

Gavin stepped toward the temporary wall. "I really like this one," he pointed to my favorite graphic. "I've never seen anything like it."

"Thanks," I replied, taken aback. My stuff had gotten little more than a cursory glance and nod for most of the evening. Gavin cocked his head slightly at me, studying my face.

"I didn't realize how talented you were," he said. I smiled shyly and could feel my cheeks burn a shade darker. They stayed chatting for a few more minutes and left when our advisor announced that the show would be closing in five minutes.

"See you tomorrow," Piper called as they walked away. Gavin's eyes lingered on me for a moment before he followed the other two out of the room.

Once home, I knocked on Mom's door. "Come in," she called back. I climbed up on the bed next to her. Her normally pristine strawberry hair was matted and the bags under her eyes were heavy.

"Mama," I said softly. "What happens next?" She stared at me sadly for a moment.

"I'm not sure, honey." She shook her head. "I think the first thing that I need to do is find a job. Nothing has been worked out. I haven't spoken to your father since that day. I don't know what is going to happen. I'm so sorry, sweetheart."

"Okay," I said slowly. She studied me, her eyes red and damp.

"Tomorrow," she said slowly.

"Tomorrow, what?" I asked, confused.

"Tomorrow we start over. Will you help me?" I had never heard my strong, confident mother speak like this. She never needed help, unless it was with the laundry or the yard work. I leaned over and wrapped my arms around her. She pulled me down next to her and pulled me close. "I

think we need some Pride and Prejudice *tonight, don't you?" she asked. I nodded, unable to speak. I hadn't snuggled with my mother like this since I was seven years old. She clicked the TV on and I tried to forget about everything but Elizabeth and Mr. Darcy.*

Just as Mr. Darcy turned up unexpectedly at Rosings, the doorbell rang. I didn't move, knowing that Whitney would answer. Sure enough, her voice called up the stairs a few minutes later. "Sydney," she called. "It's for you."

I reluctantly untangled myself from Mom's arms and went down the stairs. I stopped short at the bottom, surprised at the sight of Gavin standing there. He smiled up at me.

"Hey," I said slowly.

"Hey," he replied, holding up a cellophane bag. Chocolate covered cinnamon bears. I raised my eyebrows. "You seemed a little off tonight. I just thought you could maybe use something sweet." My mouth dropped open and I cleared the space between us and threw my arms around his neck. He wrapped his around my waist hesitantly.

"Thank you," I said softly, trying really hard to keep my emotions under control.

"Anytime," he replied, tightening his grip. "Anytime at all."

chapter three

JUNE 2017

"Aren't we going to the grad thing?" I asked as we missed the exit. Gavin smiled at me.

"Not yet." He turned his attention back to the road.

"So, where are we going?" I asked suspiciously.

"You'll see," he replied with a smile. He kept his eyes on the road and I kept my eyes on him. We had been together for three years and I still loved looking at him. He was the epitome of the boy next door, with a bright smile and a little bit of baby fat left in his cheeks. He could make me laugh with just a look.

He took the next exit and pulled onto Wasatch Boulevard in the opposite direction of Grad night.

"What are you doing?" I asked again.

"Just two more minutes." I tried to be patient as we traveled further down the road. He pulled off onto a small street that went a little bit farther up the mountain and then into a small parking lot.

He backed into a parking space and told me to stay in my seat for a minute. "Just keep your eyes on the building right there," he said, pointing straight ahead. I nodded and he climbed out of the truck. I could hear him rustling around in the bed and it killed me not to turn around. Finally he knocked on my window.

"C'mon," he said, smiling like a little boy. I jumped down from my seat and followed him to the back of the truck and stopped short. Below the parking lot the hill fell away and we had a perfect view of the valley. The sun was beginning to set over the Oquirrh mountains and I could see the lake glittering orange to the north.

"Wow," I breathed, taking it all in. It was incredible.

"C'mon," he repeated, tugging at my hand. I followed him to the back of the bed. The tailgate was open and the bed of the truck was covered by a picnic blanket. There was a small jar of flowers tucked in a corner.

"What is this?" I smiled. He pulled out a picnic basket.

"I know you went to dinner with your mom, but I thought we could have dessert." He pulled out a bag of chocolate covered cinnamon bears, chocolate covered strawberries, and a package of my favorite sugar cookies. I laughed in delight.

"Here," he said as he hopped into the back of the truck and pulled me up with him. He had some pillows arranged to make the hard truck more comfortable.

"I wondered why you borrowed your Dad's truck when you picked me up," I mused as I settled into him.

He kissed the top of my head. "I wanted to celebrate with you. I feel like we did high school together and we should end it together too."

I nestled closer to him. I couldn't have asked for anything more perfect. "Thank you, I love it." The sun dipped lower and lower in the sky turning the clouds from orange to pink to purple all the way to an inky gray. We finished the bears and made a dent in the strawberries.

"We can save the cookies for tomorrow," I suggested.

"I'm going to see you tomorrow?" he softly.

"You better. I expect to see you as much as possible all summer long."

"Yes, ma'am," he laughed, tightening his grip around me. "I will do my best."

"You always do," I replied with a kiss.

chapter four

JUNE 2014

I pressed the heels of my hands into my eyes. I would not cry anymore, I told myself. I was so tired of it and it didn't do anyone any good. I took a deep breath and steeled myself to get back to work. I taped yet another box shut and pulled out another one to fill. The majority of the move would be tomorrow and there was still so much to pack.

Dad had been gone for three months. So much had happened in that short amount of time. Dad came by the house one night and cleared out his things while the rest of us were at dinner. Mom had arranged it that way so she didn't have to see him, and we didn't have to watch him strip our home of all evidence of him. Realizing that she alone could never cover the mortgage, Mom sold the house and found one to rent that would keep us all in the same schools and that would allow us some luxuries, like food and heat. I understood the logistics of it all and I was happy that she had pulled it all off so quickly. But leaving the house that I had grown up in was proving more difficult than I had anticipated.

13

And now I was pulling all of my shoes out of my closet and throwing them into the box. As soon as I was done in here, I had to go help Tyler with his room. Mom was packing up the kitchen and Whitney was helping her. I closed the box and stood up to stretch. I stacked two boxes together and brought them downstairs. The pile along the front hallway was growing. I could feel tears prickling behind my eyes again and pushed them back with a quick shake of my head. I turned to go back up the stairs, but the doorbell rang.

"Piper!" *I said in surprise as I opened it. She was wearing an old T-shirt and shorts. Sean and Gavin were behind her similarly clothed. Gavin held two huge pizza boxes and Sean had a box of donuts.*

"Hi," *she replied brightly.* "What do you need us to do?"

I looked at her, confused. "You know we're not actually moving until tomorrow, right?"

"I know," *she replied.* "But you have to pack tonight, right?" *I nodded.* "We're here to help." *She pushed past me into the house.* "Is your room done?" *she asked. I shook my head. She took off up the stairs without another word. Gavin and Sean waited quietly for my instructions.*

"You guys didn't need to come," *I said.*

Sean shrugged. "Of course we did," *he smiled.* "You want me to go help Piper?"

"Sure," *I agreed, then I looked at Gavin.*

"Do you want to eat first or pack first?" *he asked.*

"I think Tyler would kill me if I said pack first."

"Let's eat then," *he replied, slipping past me into the house. Once the pizzas and most of the donuts had disappeared, Gavin followed me up the stairs.*

"You want to help me pack up my little brother's room?" *I asked.*

"I would love to," *he replied with a smile. With three extra sets of hands we finished hours before expected.*

"I don't know what to say," *Mom said, smiling at my friends.* "We would have been up all night without you three."

"Happy to do it, Mrs. M," *Piper replied. Sean and Gavin nodded. I walked them out to the car and gave them all a hug.*

"Thank you so much, guys. It really, really means a lot to me," *I gushed, once again trying to restrain the tears.*

"No problem," Sean and Gavin said in chorus and climbed into the car. Piper lingered a moment longer.

"Just because I think you should know, this was all Gavin's idea," she informed me with a smile.

"What?" I asked.

"He suggested we bring food and come over to help tonight. And tomorrow morning." She shrugged. "Do with that information what you will." She threw me a little wave and climbed into the car. I stood on the curb processing for a few minutes after they were out of sight.

It took a few weeks to really get settled in the new house. It was a great little house and our neighbors were kind, but it wasn't quite the same. I missed our yard, I missed our neighbors, and I missed my big closet. The one thing that made up for it was the swing that the owners left on the front porch. It was the most comfortable wooden swing that I had ever been on and was my new favorite place to read. Many nights after dinner, Mom would join me out there. Tonight was one of those nights.

I was about halfway through Ender's Game when she sat down next to me. "Is it any good?" she asked.

"Mmmhmm," I nodded, too caught up in the story to do more than that.

"Sydney?"

"Yeah?" I said without looking up. They were facing two armies in the battle room. I was not pleased with the interruption.

"Sydney," she repeated a little more sternly, "I need to talk to you about something."

"'Kay," I replied, still not looking up.

"Sydney." This time the irritation in her voice overrode my desire to find out what happened next. I looked up at her, still annoyed at being pulled out of Dragon Army like this. "We need to talk about what is going to happen next."

"So, talk."

She bit back a retort and continued. "I've been accepted to nursing school. I start in the fall." My eyes widened. I had no idea my mom wanted to be a nurse. After Dad took off she got a job at a department store, which had kept food on the table until he agreed to start helping out with the bills. They still hadn't officially signed the papers yet.

"Oh," I replied stupidly. "Okay."

"Tyler will be in school most of the day, so it shouldn't be too much of a problem, but I need you to make sure that you're home before he is. The school is close enough now that he can walk home and I talked to the Meriweathers down the street. They're happy to have Ty walk with their kids. But I won't get home until later in the evenings."

"I can do that," I nodded.

"That, and I'll need to keep my job. Try and work out my schedule around my classes or vice versa. So, starting in a couple of months, I'll be home a lot less."

"Okay," I said slowly, processing what this would mean. Mom filled in the blanks.

"I'll really need you and Whitney to step things up around here. We'll put together a schedule, but you'll need to make dinner a couple of times a week. And the two of you will have to work out your school activities and work schedule so that someone can be home with Tyler or you can take him with you." She sighed. "I know it's a lot to ask of you, sweetie, and I'm sorry to do it. It's not fair that you have to grow up overnight like this." She glanced up at me and held my eyes in hers. "But I can't do it without you."

I nodded. "Of course. Whatever you need, Mom." She reached over and gave me a hug.

"Thank you, sweetheart. I love you," she murmured close to my ear.

"I love you too." She pulled back and stood up.

"I need to go talk to Whitney now." She smiled down at me. "Thank you for being so incredible." I nodded and offered her a smile and she disappeared inside. I tried to return to my book but couldn't focus. She was right. It wasn't fair. High school wouldn't be what I had expected. Art shows, football games, dances. They would all have to be scheduled around Whitney and Tyler. A wave of bitterness washed over me. Mostly at my Dad for leaving us like this. Everything was fine before he left. Sure, he was a no-show kind of Dad, but at least he financed Mom's presence. Things were easier. I blew out my frustration. Being mad about it wouldn't do any good. I jumped as a door slammed inside the house.

Whitney was obviously not taking the news as well as I had. I curled my knees up onto the bench and lay down, leaning my suddenly heavy head against the armrest.

chapter five

JUNE 2017

Sunlight streamed suddenly onto my face. I winced and moaned aloud. "Time for breakfast!" An unexpectedly deep voice said. I peered under heavy eyelids and then groaned again.

"Why are you here? What time is it?"

James stood in the middle of my bedroom, a stupid grin on his face. "It's almost ten. I'm taking you to breakfast."

I closed my eyes and pulled the blanket over my head. I had gone to bed around five this morning. The school or the PTA or someone rented out a local family fun center for the senior class grad night. The five of us had spent the night together roller skating, driving bumper cars, and playing arcade games, and Gavin had dropped me off at sunrise.

"I'm still sleeping," I announced. "Go away." I felt a heavy weight on my legs and peeked out from under the blanket. James was sitting on my legs, determined to torture me out of bed. I muttered a few

18

obscenities under my breath as I threw the blanket back and tried to push him off of me. I fell back onto the bed feigning weakness.

"How did you even get in here?" I moaned.

"Your mom let me in. I think she wants you out of bed. She was pretty happy to see me."

"She would," I muttered. "Why are you doing this to me?" I whined. "I need to sleep."

"You're the one that wanted to do this and insisted repeatedly that I come get you." He readjusted himself on my calves.

I opened my eyes all the way for the first time and studied him. "Are you serious?"

"Yep," he nodded.

I was starting to lose feeling in my legs. I pushed him half-heartedly again. "Get off. Get out. I'll get dressed."

James slid off my bed. "Or I could just stay right here," he suggested.

"Out, sicko," I barked, pushing him toward the door.

"It was worth a try," he shrugged, as I slammed my bedroom door in his face.

XXX

He took me to our standard diner. The breakfast rush was mostly over and we found a place to sit right away. As we slid into the booth I glanced around. "Is everyone else meeting us here?" I looked at James, slightly confused. He shook his head.

"You were pretty adamant about just the two of us going." He unfolded the menu on the table and began perusing.

I narrowed my eyes at him. "There are a lot of things that you seem to remember that I don't."

A silly grin flitted across his face and his cheeks grew slightly pink. "There is a possibility that you were not entirely awake while you were talking."

"Explain," I demanded.

"You were kind of half asleep." He studied me. "You don't remember this at all?"

19

"Help me out," I requested, dryly.

"You can't remember anything," James muttered. He pursed his lips. "After we finished roller skating, you didn't want to play miniature golf."

I nodded. "I remember that."

"Okay. You asked if I wanted to stay with you. So, I did."

I conjured an image of the two of us on a padded bench, James's long legs stretched out, his head leaning against the wall behind him. I took up the rest of the bench, my head in his lap, my knees curled into me to fit on the bench. "Okay."

"I don't know at what point you actually fell asleep. You seemed pretty lucid when you were talking about breakfast."

"So I insisted you come get me for breakfast?" He nodded. "Why didn't I want anyone else to come?"

A funny look crossed his face so quickly that I thought I might have imagined it. He shrugged. "You were beginning to make less sense by then."

"How long did you let me go on for?" I asked, instantly horrified.

James smiled. "Long enough."

I looked at him, humiliated. "What else did I say?"

The waitress interrupted our conversation at that moment, took our orders quickly, and disappeared again. "At one point you were obviously dreaming." He began shredding his napkin with the fork. "I couldn't understand all of it, but there was something about sliding glass doors and riding a train?"

"I can't believe you let me do that," I replied, throwing a straw wrapper at him.

James shrugged. "What should I have done, Syd? You were exhausted."

"So, I didn't say anything super embarrassing, then?" The waitress reappeared with my French toast and James's omelet. James picked up his fork and cut a corner off of his omelet and shook his head as he took a bite.

"You just want to go home and go back to sleep after this?" He asked, a hint of disappointment in his voice.

I shrugged and dumped an unnecessary amount of syrup on my French toast. "Maybe. But, I don't know. I'm up, thanks to you."

"I was going to drive up to the university later, double check a few things up there. You want to come?"

"Sure, I replied around a mouthful of bacon. "Maybe I'll fall asleep in the car, and you can blackmail me with all the stuff I admit in my sleep."

"Why do you think I asked you?" he replied with a laugh.

XXX

We spent most of the afternoon on campus. James found the registrar's office and asked his questions. As we walked from building to building, I had to take two steps to his one. His long legs carried him much more quickly than mine did. We found a fountain under a thick canopy of trees and settled down next to it with sodas purchased from the student building. The breeze off the water cooled the area nicely and I stretched my legs out in the grass.

"Have you decided what you want to major in, yet?" I asked as I gazed at all of the buildings surrounding us. It made me the littlest bit excited to begin my own college adventure. James shook his head slowly.

"My dad thinks I should go into business." he said deliberately. He did not sound excited about this prospect.

"What do you want to do?" I asked again.

"There's a lot I could do with a business degree, you know." He sounded defensive but I could hear his dad in those words.

"James," I rebuked, "it's me."

He looked at me and took a breath. "You know I want to do photography, Syd."

"So, why don't you?" I pushed.

He shrugged. "There's a lot I could do with a business degree," he repeated.

"There's a lot you could do with photography," I countered.

"Don't, Syd. I've been through this with my dad about a hundred times." He took a long drink of his soda and readjusted so his long legs were stretched out next to mine. A breeze rustled his dark hair.

"Has he seen your work?" I asked. "It's incredible. He has to know that you'll be successful."

He gave me a sad little smile. "Thanks, but it doesn't work like that at the Sorensen house."

"Well, for what it's worth, I think you're amazing." I paused a moment. "Even if you tried to get me to tell you my deep, dark secrets."

"And failed." James laughed.

I crossed my arms behind my head and lay back to look at the sky. "What do you think college will be like?" I asked.

"Better than high school, I hope," he replied shortly.

"You didn't like high school?" I asked in surprise.

He shrugged slightly. "I liked high school enough." I turned toward him and studied his face. It was long and slender with hard lines that softened when he smiled.

"High school was pretty good," I mused. "But I wouldn't mind if college was better."

"Who knows?" James said quietly. "Maybe one day we'll both end up at Cal Arts."

I sighed. "That would definitely be better than high school," I replied wistfully.

"Definitely."

chapter six

JULY 2014

What do you mean you can't make it?" I wailed over the phone. We had all volunteered to help with a community youth dance for the Fourth of July weekend. It was a big event for the community, always held the weekend before the fourth, and this year the organization had been a little shoddy. When the jobs were handed out there had been a major miscommunication leaving Piper, Sean, Gavin, and I alone to decorate thirty-five tables and hang numberless streamers across the school's gym where the dance would be held. And now Piper and Sean were bowing out at the last second.

"What do you want me to say, Sydney?" Piper asked. "My mom scored Beyonce tickets. And I'm supposed to just pass on them?"

I sighed in frustration. "Fine. Just remember me pathetically hanging crepe paper in a gym while you're dancing with the queen." I hung up the phone and decided to deal with the repercussions later. Why were people always bailing on me?

23

I walked into the dimly lit room, my arms full of plastic tablecloths, silver streamers, and cardboard stars that the dance coordinator had given me. Gavin stood alone at the far end of the room, studying the walls.

"Hey," I called. Gavin saw me with my arms full and came over to take a load.

"Is this all?" he asked, as we dumped the decorations next to the nearest wall. I shook my head.

"No, the centerpieces and table decorations are in the front hall, but we don't have to get them yet." I glanced around the gym, looking for a sign of more help. "Anyone else show?"

Gavin shook his head. "It's just the two of us," he said with a wink.

I smiled, but bit back a groan. It would take all night with just two people. He smiled back and turned to the pile of decorations on the floor.

"What first?" he asked, waiting for instructions. I scanned the pile and then surveyed the room.

"Hmm," I thought out loud. "If we hang the streamers first, we won't ruin any tables in the process."

"Sounds like a plan," Gavin nodded, reaching down to grab an armful of the silvery ribbons. I gazed across the gym and then over to Gavin. It was going to be a long night. We set up the gigantic ladder that had been left for our use and got to work. After we got started, I was almost glad that there was no one else there. Despite the fact that it was incredibly difficult to string the streamers across the gym with just the two of us, we had more fun than expected doing it. The community center advisor popped her head in once or twice over the course of the evening to check our progress, and we had to track down a janitor when the ladder jammed shut, but otherwise, we spent the time talking and laughing.

Four hours and thirty-seven minutes later, we were done, it was almost 1:00 a.m. and we had passed exhaustion into the advanced stages of silliness. We both sat on the floor, leaning against the wall and admiring our handiwork. The stinky gym had been transformed. Stars glittered from the ceiling and tiny mirrors on all of the tables reflected the lights, casting a shimmer on the rafters. Gavin and I sat on the floor, giggling in exhaustion at things that weren't very funny. Finally, Gavin stood. "We should get home. You'll be too tired to enjoy this tomorrow if we don't." He reached out, took my hand, and pulled me to my feet. He pulled a little too hard, and I ended up almost tackling him. He steadied me and we stood there for a moment laughing. He cocked an eyebrow at me. "You sure you can bike home in this condition?"

I giggled and staggered away from him, feigning drunkenness. "What are you talking about, officer?" I slurred, "I'm totally fine to drive." And then, accidentally but appropriately, I tripped over an empty box, reached out for the nearest chair for balance, and brought it down with me. I lay on the floor, laughing hysterically. I took great gulps of air as Gavin hurried over to see if I was okay.

"Okay, that's it. I'm taking you home," he insisted, reaching down to pull me up.

"No, but—" I tried to protest through the laughter, but Gavin wouldn't let me.

"If you can't walk, there is no way you can ride a bike."

I swallowed the last few giggles. "But my bike," I began.

"We'll throw it in my trunk." Gavin pulled me to my feet again and led me out to his car, this time refusing to release my hand. We were quiet as we drove home. When we pulled in the driveway, I flashed Gavin a smile.

"I guess I will see you in the morning," I said as I reached for the door handle.

"Goodnight, Sydney," he said with a smile. I glanced back at him and, on a whim, I quickly gave him a peck on the cheek. His eyes widened and so did my smile as I hopped out of the car and waved goodbye.

XXX

Even though I had seen it the night before, I was impressed the next day with the amazing job that we had done in the gym with the decorations. Sunlight still streamed through the windows as guests began to arrive and reflected off of the mirrors and silver streamers, and the brick walls were covered with the dancing light. I stood in the doorway taking it all in and mentally patting myself on the back.

"It looks even better in the daylight, doesn't it?" asked a quiet voice next to me. I glanced over to see Gavin admiring the room as well, looking quite handsome in a dark purple polo. I nodded with a smile. "You did good, Morris."

"Well," I amended, slipping my arm through his, "I had a little bit of help. But just a little," I teased with a laugh. He led me to Sean and Piper. As we approached, I saw Piper's eyebrows rise and her eyes linger on my arm through Gavin's. I greeted them with a slightly goofy grin on my face, which remained through most of the evening.

Late that night, after everyone had gone home and the silver streamers were overflowing the dumpsters behind the school, Gavin and I watched the fireworks display from the parking lot. "Sydney?" He broke the silence after a few minutes.

"Yeah?"

"I've been thinking about you lately," he said quietly. "A lot."

"Oh?" I replied, heat creeping up my neck and blossoming across my cheeks.

"I've been wondering what it might be like to kiss you." His voice was soft. Shy.

"Oh," I breathed, unsure how to respond. "I, um, I'd like to know too."

"Okay," he replied quietly. I looked over at him and he brushed his lips gently across mine. I took a quick breath, but didn't move. He kissed me again, and I leaned into him, kissing him back.

"Are you guys coming?" Sean's voice echoed through the empty parking lot. The shout startled both of us and we pulled apart quickly. "I've got a trunk full of fireworks. Let's go!"

chapter seven

JUNE 2017

Much to my mother's dismay, I was still in bed at ten when my phone rang. Gavin didn't usually call me from his work. "Hey," he said.

"Hey, yourself," I replied, smiling. Our work schedules complicated our relationship this summer. We had weekends together, but it seemed without fail that the days that he was off, I had to work. It was the first time that I had talked to him in a couple of days and it was nice to hear his voice. For a moment.

"So, it turns out I'm going to have to work late tonight. Anthony just called in sick, and my dad wants me to stick around. So, we'll just have to postpone your birthday dinner until tomorrow, okay?" I could hear the note of regret in his voice, but resented that it was only a note.

"Oh," I replied, annoyed and disappointed. "Right, okay."

"See you then!" That was it, and he hung up. I put my phone down and stared dejectedly at the wall. That was not how my birthday was supposed to go.

I like to think of myself as a pretty easy-to-please kind of girl. But, I couldn't help but be upset. It was my eighteenth birthday. A girl doesn't turn eighteen every day. Luckily, Mom made a big deal out of it, like she usually does, making me my favorite breakfast, but other than that, not a single person had said *happy birthday* to me today. And now, I had literally nothing to look forward to. I had made my mom plan any birthday celebrations around my date with Gavin, and therefore, nothing else was planned for the rest of the day.

I had just gone into full-blown woe-is-me mode, and pulled a pint of Haagen-Dazs out of the freezer when there was a knock on the front door. I set the ice cream on the counter and padded morosely to the entryway, expecting it to be a delivery man or one of Whit's friends. I pulled the door open and found James standing there with a small birthday cake complete with candles.

"Happy Birthday!" he announced, holding the cake out to me. I smiled in spite of myself.

"C'mon in," I opened the door wider to let him pass. He set the cake down on the kitchen counter.

"What do you think?" he asked. "Should I find the matches or the forks?" He spotted the Haagen-Dazs on the counter and glanced back at me. "It looks like you were going to get started without me," he joked, his voice laced with concern. He was well aware that ice cream was my drug of choice.

"I just knew you were coming," I hedged. "I'm psychic like that." I pulled open the silverware drawer and handed him a fork.

"How does it feel to be eighteen?" he asked, leaning down to scoop out a bite of cake.

"Kind of crappy, actually," I replied, raising my fork to my lips. He furrowed his eyebrows, his mouth too full of cake to ask the question. "Birthdays are so much better when you're a little kid," I mused. "Everyone makes a big deal out of it. The presents are more exciting and people treat you differently. Now, it's just your average day, with the occasional present, like a book. A phone, if you're lucky. No more parties, no more balloons." I dug my fork violently back into the cake in front of me. James stared at me silently for a moment. I offered him a wry smile and realized how bitter I must sound. "But hey, I still get cake, right?" I held up my loaded fork like a toast before shoveling it into my mouth.

"Seriously, Syd, are you okay?" he asked, laying his fork on the counter.

"Fine," I replied shortly. "Just acting like a spoiled brat."

"Anything I can do?"

I gestured to the cake in front of me. "You brought me a cake, James. You win the prize for not sucking today." I shook my head. "I'm sorry," I murmured. "You don't have to stay here and listen to me whine."

"I'm sorry, Syd. Happy birthday, anyway." He picked his fork back up and licked off the frosting.

I smiled wryly. "Thanks."

"Hey," he said, digging back into the cake. "You have plans tonight?"

I shook my head. "Nope," I replied, bitterly.

"Well, let's hang out. We'll do something fun. I'll text you tonight, okay?"

I shrugged. "Whatever."

"Great," he responded, all of a sudden in a hurry. "I've got to go, but I'll see you tonight. Happy birthday!" He set his fork in the sink and hurried out of the kitchen.

I spent the rest of the afternoon moping. I spent some quality time channel surfing and then killed a couple hours on the internet. Since I had planned on going to dinner with Gavin that night, Mom didn't have anything special planned. She apologized several times over the tacos. By the time 7:00 rolled around, I was ready to go curl up in bed and feel sorry for myself. I was seriously contemplating that course of action when James texted me.

Hey, want to come over
and watch a movie or
something?

I figured I could mope just as easily in front of a movie as I could in my own bed, so I replied in the affirmative and drove to James's house.

I knocked on the front door and waited an unusually long amount of time before the door swung open. James stood there with a goofy grin on his face.

"Hey," he said, welcoming me inside. "Piper and Sean are already here. We were just deciding what to watch." I nodded and followed him through the kitchen and into the living room. As I came around the kitchen table, about twenty people jumped out from their hiding places and yelled, "Surprise!"

I stumbled backward, caught off guard, and ran into a chair. Due to my inherent lack of grace, it almost took me down. James caught my arm and steadied me, laughing.

"Happy birthday," he said in a low voice, keeping his hand on my arm. I flashed him an enormous smile and threw my arms around his neck.

"You are the best," I said into his ear. "Thank you." I pulled away, still smiling, and turned to the rest of my friends. "Thanks, you guys!" I made the rounds, greeting everyone, passing out hugs.

After about an hour of laughing and talking, Sean ducked out of the room and returned seconds later carrying a huge balloon bouquet and Piper followed close behind, a giant cake in her arms.

"Let's eat!" yelled one of the boys. Everyone headed for the table where Piper had set the cake. James held up his hands, holding them off.

"No one eats until we sing," he announced, producing candles and matches. I laughed as I was ushered ceremoniously to the table. James was meticulous and lit eighteen candles before moving out of my way. The crowd sang a loud and rousing rendition of "Happy Birthday," and as I leaned forward to blow out the candles, James leaned in close to me.

"Don't forget to make a wish," he advised with a smile. I smiled and turned back to somehow blow out every single one of those eighteen candles in one breath.

The party was a blast. Piper pulled out "Battle of the Sexes" and the girls won, hands down, but I have a theory that there may have been a conspiracy in play to let us win. Around 11:00 that night, most of the guests had trickled out and James turned on a movie. I collapsed on the couch next to James and glanced around the room. Piper was almost asleep next to Sean on the loveseat, Will was on the floor, leaning against the couch and Beth's legs, where she sat on the other side of James. I turned my attention to the movie. *The Princess Bride.* My favorite.

"Happy birthday," James whispered, poking me in the ribs. I smiled and leaned my head on his shoulder. "So what did you wish for?" he asked.

"I'm not telling you what I wished for!" I whispered back in mock horror. "Then it won't come true!"

I felt his chest rise with a small chuckle. "No, see, everyone thinks that's how it works, but really the rule is you can only tell one person. If you tell more than one, then you're out of luck and it won't, but one person is fine. Especially if it's me."

I glanced up to find a mischievous grin on his face. I smiled back at him.

"I wished that next year you would still be around to make my birthday not suck," I whispered. He shifted his arm, putting it around my shoulders. "As you wish," he answered.

chapter eight

SEPTEMBER 2014

The first time that I met James it was my very first day of tenth grade. He sat behind me in Sophomore English. When I walked into class on the first day, I glanced around the room and quickly realized that I didn't know a single person in there. I sat in the first empty seat I saw, closest to the door and right in front of a tall boy with curly dark hair. His legs were so long that they didn't quite fit under the desk and one stretched out into the aisle. I slid into the chair and reached into my backpack, rustling through my papers, trying to cover the fact that I had no one to chat with before class started. It was my second year of high school and even though I knew my way around for the most part, I was still as uneasy as I had been that morning. A lot had changed over the summer and I wasn't sure how that would affect my life once school was again in session.

When I pulled my head out of my backpack, James leaned forward and spoke. *"You're here for Advanced Calculus, right?"* I whirled around *in terror. It had been a very long day already, and if I was in the wrong class, I might just have a nervous breakdown. As soon as I saw the smile on his face, though, I knew that was not the case. I scowled at him.*

"You know, you could have just said, 'Hi, it's nice to meet you,'" I scolded, turning back around to face the board. I could feel his breath on the back of my neck as he leaned forward to talk to me.

"I could," he said, "but my way is so much more fun," he laughed. I turned back to roll my eyes at him.

"I'm James," he said, his smile slightly apologetic.

"Sydney."

"Hi, Sydney. It's nice to meet you." He exaggerated the sentiment with a slight bow of the head. He kept his eyes on me, waiting for a reaction.

"See how much better that was?"

He shrugged and cocked an eyebrow at me. "Not really." I had just enough time to shoot him the evil eye before class began.

And that was the way most of the year went. James teasing, me scolding, with an occasional role reversal. I didn't know it then, but that would be the seating arrangement for the rest of the year. We had a great teacher—impatient, but great. Well, I thought so, anyway. James and Mr. Thompson shared an intense mutual dislike, aided by James's tendency to be just a bit of a know it all. The majority of the class thought his comments were funny. Mr. Thompson did not. James spent plenty of time hating Mr. Thompson, and I spent plenty of time listening to him vent.

According to the seating arrangement, we were divided into study groups. Within a few months, James and I began staying late after study group to talk, go get ice cream, and just hang out. We realized that he had moved into my new neighborhood about the same time that I had. He was a natural addition to the four of us. He got along great with Gavin and even better with Sean. We partnered up on our final project, an oral report on The Odyssey. *We finished it quickly and spent the rest of the allotted in-class work time playing "Would You Rather?" and avoiding Mr. Thompson's death stare.*

"Would you rather have invisibility and teleportation powers, or the ability to read minds and fly?" James asked the first question.

I looked at him like he was crazy. "Hello, invisibility and teleportation. Because if you can teleport, who needs flying?"

"True," James agreed, nodding, "but you wouldn't want to read minds?"

I shook my head. "If I could be invisible, then I could just eavesdrop on everyone, which would solve most of my problems." I grinned. "Your turn: would you rather compete in the Triwizard Tournament or the Hunger Games?"

"Triwizard Tournament. That's not even a question. The losers of the Tournament don't die."

"They do if they're Cedric Diggory."

"I'll take those odds." James paused, "You know, we're nerds," he posited thoughtfully.

"It's what makes this friendship work. Oooh, here's one: would you rather date your favorite celebrity or your crush?"

"I'm pretty sure it's my turn," James pouted.

"Just answer and then you can ask me two." I gave him my best puppy dog eyes.

James sighed. "What if they are the same?"

"Doesn't count."

"My crush," he replied after a while.

"Really?" I exclaimed in surprise. James shrugged.

"They are both equally unattainable."

"I am very curious about this 'unattainable' crush," I teased. "I think you should tell me about it."

James laughed. "That is not how this game works."

"Oh, c'mon. Maybe I can set you up!" I poked his arm obnoxiously. "It'll be fun!"

He just shook his head at me. "What about you?" he asked. "Celebrity or crush?"

"If Chris Evans was available, I think I might just have to go down that road."

"Who?"

"Captain America?" I responded, annoyed at his ignorance. "Mmm. Him or Ryan Reynolds." I gave an exaggerated sigh and stared off into space. He poked my arm and I wrinkled my nose at him.

"Fine," I said, "would you rather have your crush date your best friend or your worst enemy?"

"See, I swear it's my turn again."

"You know you want to answer. C'mon."

"You're impossible."

"I know." I gave him my most charming smile.

"Worst enemy," James said, without having to think about it.

"Why?" I asked.

"I wouldn't feel bad at all if I managed to steal her out from under his nose."

I nodded sagely. "Smart," I said with a smile.

chapter nine

June 2017

What days are you working again?" Mom asked as she packed her lunch. She was working three back-to-back shifts starting in the morning. Twelve on, twelve off for the next three days. When she did that, we only saw her for about an hour or two of her twelve home, she slept the rest. Whitney and I held down the fort and got Tyler everywhere that he needed to be. It was a little easier in the summer; we didn't have to make sure he had a ride to school.

"I work tomorrow, Wednesday, and Friday," I replied. "They have some corporate thing Thursday that I don't need to be at, so I get the day off." I was really looking forward to taking full advantage of that day.

"Do you know Whitney's schedule?" Whitney was working a part time job at the same community center I had worked at for the past couple of years.

"I think she has mornings this week, and I'm pretty sure she's on this weekend." She was out with her friends, or I would have tracked her down to ask. "I can text her and double check."

"Please do." Mom pulled out her own phone and opened her calendar. "So, Tyler will need somewhere to go Wednesday and Friday morning, correct?"

"If I'm right about her schedule, yep." I was still waiting for a reply.

"Okay. I'll text the Meriweathers and the Bronsons—" she was cut off by a loud yell.

"NO!" Tyler came running into the room. Living in a smaller house was a double-edged sword. Sound carried so much better here. "I DON'T want to go to the Bronsons'!" He was out of breath from his sudden burst of exertion.

"What?" Mom asked, dismayed. "You love playing with Derek."

"No I don't!" he replied emphatically. "Derek is stupid."

"Tyler," Mom rebuked him gently. "That's not very nice."

"Derek's not very nice," he shot back.

Mom studied him for a moment. "I'll try and see if you can go to the Bradshaws', but if they're not around, I'm sorry, sweetie, but you'll probably have to go to Derek's." Tyler made a face at her. "I promise I will do my best. Why don't you go get ready for bed?" Tyler sulked out of the room. Mom watched him go with concern.

"Do you know what happened?" she asked softly. I shrugged. I did know, but I would do just about anything to not have to tell her. "Did they get in a fight?" she pressed.

"I'm sure it's not that big of a deal," I stared at my hands, unable to look her in the face. "It'll probably blow over quick." I glanced up at her, trying to gage her reaction. She wasn't buying it.

"Do you know what happened, Sydney?" Mom had this way of speaking softly that was very, very terrifying. It didn't matter that I had just turned eighteen. It made me feel like a seven-year-old caught with a bag of Halloween candy under her pillow.

"Derek said some things that hurt Tyler's feelings." It was not a lie. Mom zeroed in on me. "He asked why we had to move. And why Dad didn't live with us anymore." Mom's face fell. I hated this.

"What else?" she pressed. She was well aware that those were questions that Tyler got on a regular basis.

I sighed. "Derek said that because Tyler didn't have a dad anymore, that made him a bastard. I guess his older brother read it in a book and told him what it meant." Mom let out an audible gasp. I hurried on. "Mrs. Bronson was super apologetic when I picked him up. I don't know if she heard Derek say it or if Tyler told her, but she apologized a dozen times and told me that Derek would be grounded from like everything."

"Tyler was really upset, wasn't he?" she asked quietly. I nodded. "Why didn't he tell me?"

I shrugged. "He didn't want to hurt you. I talked to him about it. He didn't want me to tell you about it either. He was trying to protect you."

Mom bit her lip and turned away from me. I knew she was crying and I knew she didn't want me to see. I felt a wave of anger at Dad. All of this was his fault. All of it. Mom opened a cabinet opposite me and began rustling the contents without paying attention.

"Could you find my purple water bottle for me, Sydney, please?" She spoke without turning around. I hopped off the stool.

"Sure," I replied, happy to give her the minute to regain her composure. If Dad hadn't left, this would not be happening. Mom would be home with Tyler. He would not know what the word *bastard* meant. Well, maybe he would, but he wouldn't be trying to apply it to himself. Mom would not be crying in the kitchen of this tiny house. It had been over three years and if I didn't think about it, I was fine. But moments like this, moments when everything goes back to him, I can barely stand it.

I spent much longer than necessary rummaging through Mom's purse and when I had returned to the kitchen, water bottle in hand, her eyes were dry and she was placing the last plastic container into her lunch tote. "Thank you, sweetheart," she said as she took the water bottle from me and filled it with ice.

"Do you want me to go grocery shopping on Thursday?" I asked as she screwed the lid back on. She looked up at me gratefully.

"Sydney, that would be wonderful. I'll text you the list tomorrow on my break, if I can remember." She grabbed my hand and squeezed it quickly. "Sometimes I just don't know what I would do without you." I shot her a smile and pulled away. I escaped to my room and shut the door, my heart sinking. Maybe going away to college would be harder than I thought.

chapter ten

MAY 2017

We had all received our college acceptance letters within a few days of each other and decided to celebrate.

"Dinner up in the canyon?" James suggested hopefully. I was all for it. Roasted hot dogs followed by s'mores? The smell of campfire and aspen trees? What could be better? Other, more refined personalities, however, didn't agree.

"Too dirty," announced Piper. "This is a real celebration. How about La Caille?" All four of us looked at her in disbelief and started laughing. Piper would suggest the most expensive restaurant in the valley. "What?" she protested. "It's great for a celebration!"

"Yeah," I retorted, swallowing the last of my laughter, "if you're a millionaire."

"Fine," she pouted.

"The Roof is good too," suggested Gavin. "Or Log Haven." James and I winced. The price was still much too high for either of us.

"What about a party?" Sean suggested, trying to smooth things over. "Cheaper, plus we're not the only ones with acceptance letters to celebrate."

Piper clapped her hands in delight. "Perfect," she said. "We can have it at my house. This weekend?"

I shrugged. It was better than blowing my savings on a single dinner. "I'm in."

XXX

The party that weekend was much bigger than any of us were expecting. Apparently, word spread far past the thirty or so seniors that we invited. Luckily, she lived in one of the largest homes in the area.

"This is way better than a prim and proper dinner," she shouted to me over the blaring music. "I don't know why I didn't think of it in the first place!"

After making the rounds at least twice, I was disinclined to agree with Piper, but I nodded anyway. She danced off through the crowd to talk to someone else. Gavin and Sean had disappeared a while ago. I glanced around the room, looking for an appealing conversation to join, but it was loud, it was hot, and I desperately needed a breath of fresh air. I slowly squeezed my way through the crowd and finally reached the front door. The music trailed after me, but the heat stayed trapped inside. I took deep, cleansing breaths of fresh air. It was early May, and while the days were beautiful and warm, the nights still had a little bite to them. I sat on a red Adirondack chair on the front porch, drinking in the clean air and admiring the nearby towering mountains when the door opened again, and James burst out, escaping from the party as well.

"Had enough?" I asked. James turned in surprise at the sound of my voice and sunk into the chair next to me.

"You know, I'm not usually claustrophobic, but there are way too many people in there." He ran his fingers through his dark hair and fought off a little shiver as he settled into his chair.

"Agreed," I nodded. I leaned my head back against the chair and propped my feet up on the porch railing as I looked up at the stars. This close to the mountain, just far enough away from the majority of the city *lights, the stars were gorgeous and bright. I traced the big dipper with my eyes.*

"You nervous?" I asked, glancing over at him. His long legs stretched out in front of him and he kept his eyes skyward as he answered.

"About what?"

"College. Leaving home. You know." I spun my hair around my hand, pulling it off my neck.

"Oh," he shifted in his seat, his eyes falling on me. He chuckled faintly. "No. I'm not actually leaving home."

I had forgotten that he'd live at home and winced slightly. "I mean for classes," I amended quickly.

"Not especially. Are you?"

I shrugged and piled my copper hair on top of my head. "I'm not nervous. Maybe I was a little concerned, but that's not the same thing," I glanced at James, wondering if he caught the movie reference, and by his exaggerated eye roll, I'm pretty sure he did. "But really," I began again with a smile, "not so much about the school part of it, more about the money and the housing and the roommates. I'm worried about my mom and Tyler and Whitney." I paused a moment before continuing. "But I think I'm ready for it." I paused briefly. "I want to get lost," I added, softly, my eyes still on the mountains.

"Hmm?" James turned to me, confusion on his face.

"I've lived here all of my life. I know where every street goes. I can get around here with my eyes closed. I want to go somewhere that I can get lost." I'm not sure where all of that came from, but I glanced at James, wondering if he thought I was completely crazy.

He was quiet. After a few moments he turned toward me, studying me. I smiled slightly hoping he wasn't about to suggest I be institutionalized when the door banged open.

"What are you doing out here, Morris?" Gavin swaggered over, flushed from the heat of the party. He looked between James and me. "You two are the only people worth my time, and you're hiding out on the porch?" The smile on his face betrayed his exaggeration.

"What?" I exclaimed in mock protest. "I am so telling Piper you said that," I teased. Gavin's eyes widened and he held his hands up in surrender.

"Joking," he declared. "Totally joking. Piper might eviscerate me for that one."

I clicked my tongue at him. "Such a coward," I bantered. "Afraid of a girl."

Gavin laughed. "Piper, just a girl," he chuckled. "I'm telling her you said that!'

"Okay, okay, truce," I laughed.

"Oh, no," Gavin replied with mock severity. "You're not getting off that easily." I raised my eyebrows at him, wondering what would come next. "You owe me a dance, Sydney," he announced, holding out his hand to pull me out of my chair. I put my hand in his with a laugh.

"You're on," I smiled as I got to my feet. Gavin led me inside. As we walked through the door, I glanced back at James, still sitting in the Adirondack. "You coming?"

James shook his head. "Not yet," he said simply, turning his focus back to the sky. The cool night breeze swirled around my face and I took one last deep breath of fresh air as I ducked inside.

chapter eleven

JULY 2017

The biggest benefit of Mom's job was that she couldn't hound me out of bed on my days off. She hated it when I stayed up too late and then wasted a day in bed. "It just makes more sense to be awake with the sun," she would say, shaking her head at me. I would remind her that she was a teenager once too, and she would shoot back with some story about how Grandpa would make her get up and do yard work every Saturday morning.

This morning I lazed around until almost eleven before showering. Tyler liked days like this as well. He could eat as much cereal as he liked while watching more cartoons than Mom would ever permit. I jumped in the shower when I remembered my promise to Mom to go grocery shopping and picked up my phone. Gavin had to work all day, so I texted James and asked if he wanted to come along.

"Hey, Ty, are you dressed?" I asked as I pulled the last carton of yogurt out of the fridge.

"No." I was lucky to even get a response when his eyes were so glued to the TV.

"Go get dressed; we have to go grocery shopping." I sat at the counter and pulled the top off my breakfast.

"Sydney," he whined, "I want to watch this!"

"You've seen this one," I commented as Phineas and Ferb chased a mummy. "I've seen this one. Go get dressed. James is coming." Tyler's head swiveled around.

"Really?"

"Yep."

Tyler jumped up and ran down the hall to his room. He was back and dressed in minutes. Of all my friends, he liked James the best. Piper was "rude," Sean was "boring," and Gavin was "kind of weird." But James played basketball with him sometimes and had let Tyler win every single game of "Mario Kart" that they had ever played. We swung by James's house and picked him up on the way.

"Can I hold the list?" Tyler asked as we got out of the car.

"It's on my phone," I replied hesitantly. I did not want to set Tyler loose with my phone in the grocery store.

"What if Ty and me take the list, and you go get all the fruit and stuff?" James suggested. I shrugged. I did trust him more than Tyler.

"Okay. I'll meet you . . ."

"In the ice cream aisle?" Tyler suggested with a wide smile. I laughed.

"Sure. I will meet you in the ice cream aisle."

"Yes!" Tyler actually jumped in the air. "Let's go, James." James had to jog to catch up. I shot him a grateful look, grabbed a basket, and found all the produce my mom had requested. It wasn't long before I was staring longingly at the Haagen-Dazs display.

"Sydney, did you see these?" I turned to see Tyler pulling a box of popsicles out of a freezer door about halfway down the aisle. James was right behind him, making sure Tyler didn't knock everything off the shelf.

"What are they?" I asked, heading in their direction and complimenting myself on my willpower.

"They're four different colors, like tie dye popsicles!" Tyler announced excitedly. "Can we get them?" I glanced at the box and then at the price. Definitely no Haagen-Dazs.

"One box," I replied. "That's it." Tyler dropped the box in my basket with a smile and then had to be dragged from the aisle before he could ask for every kind of popsicle they carried.

The lines were longer than I had expected them to be in the middle of the day. Tyler entertained himself by counting candy bars in the checkout lane.

"You didn't have to work today?" I asked James. He shook his head. He worked for a print shop near the college campus.

"They accidentally overscheduled like three days this week. I'm not supposed to have today off, but there were too many of us, so they called me this morning. I've got tomorrow and Saturday off too." He didn't sound like someone who was unexpectedly given a long weekend. The opposite in fact.

"Don't get so excited," I teased. "They might ask us to leave if you can't get it under control." He laughed slightly.

"You know how it is," he replied quietly. "I need every day's salary I can get."

"I know," I replied.

"Yeah," he shook his head with a sad smile and glanced at Tyler. "Anyway. I have the whole day off. You have the whole day off. If we can't make some money, we should at least enjoy ourselves, yeah?"

"Absolutely. First, you can help me load the groceries into my car and then we can all put them away in my kitchen."

"Wow, Syd. That's probably the best idea I've heard I'll day," he laughed.

"I know. I'm *such* a good friend." He laughed harder and set his basket on the conveyor belt.

"Maybe Tyler will share one of his cool popsicles with me," he said just loud enough to get Ty's attention. Ty swiveled around.

"Are you going to come over?" Tyler asked. "We could play Xbox!"

"One of these days, Ty, I will actually beat you at 'Mario Kart.'"

Ty snorted. "Not today."

I laughed and set my basket next to James. "See?" I said. "Way better than work."

"Couldn't agree more."

chapter twelve

NOVEMBER 2015

We managed to snag our favorite corner booth, which was a major feat on a Friday night. We put in our standard order, shakes and fries, and laughed about the embarrassing excuse for a football game that we had come from. Well, except for Sean. Sean was furious that his team had embarrassed him so badly. There was really no coming back from the slaughter on the field tonight and he knew it.

"I have never seen so many interceptions in my life!" He ranted while we waited for the food to arrive. James blew a straw wrapper at me and I narrowed my eyes at him. "And to miss a field goal that close?" Sean shook his head and rolled his eyes.

"Hey," Gavin tried to interject, "at least it's only junior year. They have a whole year to get their crap together so that our class at least doesn't go out with a whimper."

James snorted. "You make it sound like graduation is death."

"If you haven't got your health, you haven't got anything," I smiled. James and I burst out laughing while the other three looked at us like we were crazy.

"Anyway," Piper said slowly, "at least we didn't make the playoffs. Now I don't have to sit through any more football games until next fall." She leaned back in her chair with a smile on her face. She came to the games but didn't love them. The only reason that she agreed to it was to see the players in uniform. That is not what she told Sean, but I was very aware of her true intentions. Piper could not pass up a pair of tight pants.

"She's right. No more football until next fall," Sean repeated dejectedly. "What are we going to do now?"

"Like right now?" I asked.

"Next weekend," Sean replied. "There's nothing to do."

"We can go to the movies," Piper suggested.

"Miniature golfing," said Gavin.

"We could go bowling." I tried.

"Hunt horcruxes," James said. I giggled and Piper smiled.

"Fight death eaters," I continued.

"Practice our patronuses," James laughed.

"Okay, nerds," Sean interrupted. "Seriously."

"What did we do last winter?" Gavin asked.

"Watched movies," Piper replied. "I'm good with that." She slid closer to Sean and smiled up at him. I made a gagging noise and she shot me a look.

"We have rules for a reason." I reminded her. "No gratuitous PDA unless the lights are off."

"Says the girl who sat on her boyfriend's lap for all of the fourth quarter," she shot back.

"It was cold," I protested to a chorus of laughter. "Fine. Just don't be super disgusting."

"We're never disgusting, are we pookie?" Sean said in a high-pitched baby voice and pulled Piper closer to him. They made loud kissing noises at each other until James punched Sean in the shoulder.

"What are you guys doing tomorrow?" James asked.

"I have to work," Gavin announced, much to my dismay.

"Me too," Sean said.

"My mom is taking me shopping," Piper squealed. "New shoes!"

"Syd?" James asked.

"I'm off for once." We rotated weekends and this was my one available Saturday. I had every intention of sleeping in as late as my mother could stand.

"I'm going up the canyon before the snow gets really bad next month. You want to come?"

My eyes lit up. The mountains were my happy place. "Of course!" I grabbed Gavin's arm. "You should try and get off early, come with us!"

Gavin shook his head. "You guys go. I'm off at eight. I can meet you somewhere when you're done."

"You never go hiking with me," I pouted.

"There's a reason for that," Gavin shot back with a little smile. To him, hiking was more trouble than it was worth.

"Fine," I wrinkled my nose at him. "What time are you going?" I asked James.

"After lunch?"

"Perfect," I replied. James was the perfect hiking buddy. He loved it more than I did and he was almost hard to keep up with. His long legs gave him a serious advantage.

"You guys should come to my house after," Piper volunteered. "I'll get my mom to order us some pizza."

"All you had to say was free food." James laughed.

"Figured," smiled Piper. She glanced around the diner. "Where are our shakes? What is taking so long?"

"I'll go check," James offered and slid out of the booth. I glanced at Gavin.

"You don't mind that James and I go hiking together? Without you?" I asked.

He looked at me funny. "Should I?" he asked. I shook my head.

"No, but some guys would."

He leaned forward and kissed me gently. "I'm not some guys."

"Nope," I agreed, kissing him again. "You are definitely not."

chapter thirteen

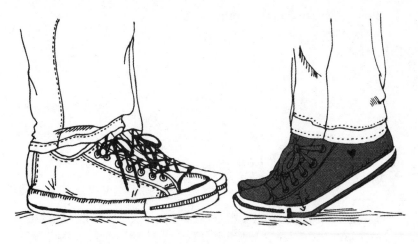

July 2017

I woke up earlier that morning than usual and couldn't fall back asleep. It was even my day off. It seemed like such a waste to be home and not be sleeping. I laid in bed for awhile, trying, but when sleep didn't come, I rolled over, grabbed my phone, and texted Gavin.

> Want to go get breakfast
> or something?

He texted back, moments later.

Sleeping.

I glanced at the clock. 7:20. Yeah. I sighed, trying to decide what to do now. I thought over my to-do list for the next few weeks, but nothing sounded appealing at all. And then it occurred to me:

James! James would be up for a run. We could go do something. I picked my phone back up.

Want to go do something?

I got a response almost immediately.

Sure. Hike?

Perfect.

I'll meet you at your house in 20.

I rolled out of bed and pulled on some shorts and hiking boots. I knew from experience that hiking with James would require a lot of water and a lunch. I pulled out a backpack and got started.

I was just finishing up the peanut butter sandwiches when there was a knock on the door. James stood there, obviously just off a run, smiling broadly. He followed me into the kitchen and offered me his opinion about what shouldn't be allowed in the backpack. When we both agreed we had a sufficient amount of food, we headed out.

As we drove, James tried to commandeer the radio. It happened every time that we were in the car together. It had gotten to the point that James made a rule: your car, your choice. He did it because he drove more often than I did, but I was not about to let him get away with breaking it today.

"Hey," I rebuked, slapping his hand away from the buttons. "My car, my choice!" I hit the volume knob and jacked it up as high as it would go before belting out the last chorus of "Shake It Off," just to drive him crazy. After my big finish, I glanced at him, hoping to rub it in even further. His head was leaning on the headrest, a small smile on his lips.

"You're impossible, you know?" he said.

"I know," I smiled, and turned the music down.

"Big or Little?" I asked, referring to the canyons. James thought about it for a few minutes, and looked back at me.

"Waterfall or lake?" he asked.

"Oooh, hard one. Hmm, lake." I decided.

"Okay, Big." So, we headed up Big Cottonwood Canyon, discussing work, friends, and college plans. "So have you found your dorm yet?" James asked.

I nodded. "We drove up for a night and went and looked at the place. It's tiny. You'd think for as much money as we're spending, we'd at least get carpet."

He glanced over at me. "No carpet? What kind of floor is it?"

"Concrete."

His mouth dropped. "That's allowed?"

I shrugged. "Apparently so. Luckily, I think between my mom and my roommates we should have enough rugs to cover at least part of it. We've been emailing for a couple of weeks."

We reached the trailhead for Lake Blanche and I was glad I brought my sweatshirt. The first half of the trail was along a creek, and although the day would be warm, the water brought the temperature down enough to be chilly.

James insisted on carrying the backpack and I followed him up the trail. I loved being up here in the morning. The sunlight was still soft, and you could almost smell the mountain waking up. I was quiet for the first little while, admiring my surroundings.

"You okay?" James finally asked, as we stopped to take a water break.

"I'm fine," I said, putting the lid back on the water bottle. "Just thinking how much I'm going to miss this when I get up to school."

He smiled. "Miss this?" he gestured to the surrounding scenery, "Or this?" His smile widened as he pointed to himself. I couldn't help smiling with him.

"Both," I said, handing him the water bottle. "But mostly, I'll miss beating you at everything," I shouted as I took off up the trail, leaving him in the dust. Between his long legs and his penchant for running, I didn't stand a chance.

"Whatever," he yelled over his shoulder. "You're going to miss getting your butt kicked! You just don't want to admit it!"

We bantered the rest of the way up the mountain, arriving at a completely deserted Lake Blanche. This was one of my favorite hikes. The lake was unnaturally still, almost a mirror of the sky. And the view was incredible. I felt like I could see forever. I stood at the edge of the lake, drinking it all in.

"I should have brought my camera," he lamented. I glanced over at him and found his eyes already on me.

"I've got my phone," I offered, pulling it out of my pocket.

"Thanks," James replied, taking it from me and beginning to snap photos. I found a flat rock nearby and sat.

"So, have you decided?" I asked as I pulled snacks out of the backpack. "Are you going to do photography?"

James lowered the phone and shook his head. "Business," he responded. I stared at him in concern.

"Will you hate it?" I asked.

He laughed wryly. "Does it matter?"

"Of course it matters!" I yelped indignantly. "I distinctly remember having a very similar conversation with you about this very subject, only then, it was about me and graphic design. And I believe your very words were: 'Syd, if you don't do it, you'll regret it for the rest of your life.'" I watched as he deliberately turned away from me and took photos of the other side of the lake. I decided that I didn't want to have this battle up here either. "I just want you to be happy, James." I paused, realizing how corny and cliché I sounded, and I decided I didn't care. "You deserve it," I added.

James turned around slowly and snapped a picture of me. I made a face at him and he took another.

"Give me back my phone!" I barked, jumping off the rock and attempting to wrench it out of his hands. He just held it higher, laughing at my pathetic attempts to reach it. I glared at him, "Fine, I take it back. You don't deserve it." He smiled at me and lowered the phone.

"One more," he promised. "Come here." I stood next to him and he held the phone at arm's length and took a selfie.

We made our way down the mountain after lunch, our conversation more substantial.

"How's everything going with Gavin?" James asked, drawing me out of my contemplation. I glanced over at him suspiciously, and almost went sprawling down the mountain, thanks to a particularly evil tree root. James grabbed my arm and steadied me before I could answer.

"Why?" I asked slowly.

"Just wondering," James said, keeping his voice and his face innocent.

"It's fine," I responded.

"What are you going to do when you both leave next month?" he asked, keeping his eyes on the trail. I kept my eyes down as well, hoping to avoid any trips to the emergency room.

"Haven't talked about it much," I said. "Kind of avoiding it to be honest. And thank you so much for bringing up a painful subject. While you're at it, why don't you give me a nice paper cut and pour lemon juice on it."

James just rolled his eyes at me. "*The Princess Bride?*"

"What else?" I smiled.

"You're a nerd."

"'No more rhymes now, I mean it!'" I teased, waiting to see if he would take the bait.

"'Anybody want a peanut?'" James laughed.

"See, you're a nerd too!"

James just shook his head. "I just spend too much time with you," he cracked. "Seriously, though. What do you want to do?"

I could hear the genuine curiosity in his voice. I shook my head. "I don't know," I replied. James glanced at me, his eyebrows raised incredulously. "No, really," I repeated. "I honestly don't know. We've been together for so long, it seems strange to just end it because we're moving, but . . ." I trailed off.

"But Yale and Boise aren't exactly close?"

"Yeah," I agreed. "We'll only see each other at Christmas, and if he decides to live at home for the summer. Everything will change no matter what."

"That's for sure. And then if you end up at Cal Arts—"

"Knock on wood," I interrupted. He smiled and continued. "That's even further."

I nodded. "At least you and Sean are only a few hours away."

He smiled at me. "Better than across the country, but still too far."

"Agreed."

I studied him for a moment. The closer the moment of goodbye got, the less I actually wanted to leave. I shook off the thought and forced a smile. "Let's not think about that today," I requested.

"Deal," he agreed. "Race you down?"

I laughed. "Not unless you want to end the day at the hospital."

He held out a hand to me to help me over a rock. "'Please consider me as an alternative to suicide.'"

"As you wish," I replied with a laugh.

chapter fourteen

MARCH 2017

The last four months of high school are completely and utterly worthless. College applications have been submitted. Fate is already in the works and a last minute failing grade in Trig is not going to change it now. It was, to say the least, a struggle to stay focused after Christmas. Luckily, I had Yearbook to keep me going. I had taken the single graphic design class Adamson High offered, along with all of the art classes, and there was nowhere to go from there. I had hoped that Yearbook would give me some opportunity to hone my skills, designing layouts or something, but, much to my initial dismay, the yearbook printers provided all the layouts. All we had to do was drag and drop. Luckily, a few weeks into the year, my yearbook advisor discovered my artistic endeavors and put me to work. She had me design custom logos for each of the clubs and teams, even procuring a better version of Photoshop for me to do it on.

Piper and James were on yearbook staff with me. James was the best photographer the yearbook had seen in a decade. Piper just thought it would be a great opportunity to get her name on every possible page in the yearbook. She did pretty well, managing to get herself on about thirty pages.

"You know," I chided, coming up behind her as she finished up the index. "If Ms. Sanford catches on, she'll delete your name entirely from the index." Piper laughed and shook her head.

"Ms. Sanford has more important things to stress about than padding the index." Piper's long chestnut ponytail bounced as she laughed.

"True," I conceded, sliding into a chair next to her. She clicked out of the index and turned to face me.

"So, there are a couple of extra blank pages at the end of the book," she confided quietly, as if she were revealing earth-shattering news.

"Yeah," I agreed. "For everyone to sign on the last day." The 'duh' was implied.

Piper shook her head. "No, more than that. We miscounted somewhere and ordered too many pages." A mischievous grin spread across her face. "Which means," she continued, "we can do whatever we want with them!"

I cocked an eyebrow at her. "What exactly are you suggesting?" I asked warily.

"We sell them," she conspired eagerly.

I laughed. "To whom?" I asked.

"I have a few ideas," she supplied slyly.

"Have you asked Sanford?" I asked, already knowing the answer.

"No," she whispered, "Not 'we' sell them," she said, pointing around to the rest of the class. "We sell them," she finished, gesturing between the two of us. She raised her eyebrows impressively and waited for a response. "What do you think?"

I shook my head in confusion. "How is this possibly going to work?" I asked skeptically. "We have to send the pages to the printer through Sanford. She has to approve everything that we send. There's no way to get it past her." I shook my head again. "You're crazy."

"No, listen, Sydney," Piper leaned closer to me. "We tell her we're putting stuff on those pages, but we don't tell her we're charging for it."

I still wasn't convinced. "What is someone going to pay to put on the last few pages of the yearbook?"

She gave me a sympathetic look and I knew she was mourning my simplistic brain. "Sydney," she said patiently, "people will pay to have their name on another page in the yearbook. We could sell personal messages. What girl wouldn't be totally thrilled to see her boyfriend's undying love printed in the yearbook underneath their picture?"

"I don't know."

"We can get James to take pictures for like twenty bucks a shot or something. I've already been asking around a little. People are all over it." I still wasn't convinced. "James!" she hissed. He turned away from the table where he was sorting the leftover photos, deciding which ones should go in the index. "Come here!"

He stood and crossed the classroom with his long legs in about three steps. "What's up?"

Piper quickly explained her plan, adding the suggestion that we could use the profits for our senior trip we had planned. James glanced between the two of us.

I sat back in my chair, looking at Piper with a new respect. "You really think it will work?" I asked again, this time seriously. She nodded solemnly.

"But I need you to help me," she added.

"Why?" I asked.

"Ms. Sanford trusts you," she replied confidentially. "She'll never go for anything that I suggest. But if it comes from you . . ." she trailed off, her meaning implied. "Plus," she added in a singsong voice, "You'll get to design the layout and everything." She dangled it in front of me like a big shiny carrot.

"What are the prices?" I asked.

"Not totally sure," she responded, thoughtfully. "Maybe like twenty dollars for a small picture, thirty for a large one? Ten dollars extra for a caption?"

"Seriously?" I hissed. "You think people will actually pay that much?"

She nodded. "I've asked around," she said. I glanced at James. He just shrugged.

I raised my eyebrows, even more impressed. "You are going to get me kicked off the staff," I shook my head at her.

"So?" she smiled. "The yearbook's already done!"

Piper brought it up again late that night at Gavin's. "Wait, what?" *Gavin asked. Piper launched into a condensed version of her plan. Gavin looked between the three of us. "Are you seriously going along with this?"*

"I did the math," Sean announced. "If we can fill up both pages, it'll pay for the trip to Cali."

Gavin looked at me. "Syd?"

I shrugged. "I don't love it. But . . ." I trailed off. The money was very, very tempting.

"James?"

"Not my call." It wasn't, but James would take every opportunity to perfect his art. We devised a plan between the five of us, all the while Gavin voicing his conscientious dissent. I suggested the idea to Ms. Sanford the next afternoon and by some incredible stroke of luck we got away with it. Piper was in charge of sales and keeping everything absolutely confidential, and I designed a two-page layout that would maximize the amount of pictures we could squeeze in. We slid it past Ms. Sanford with an incredibly professional look and then used the money to book a hotel in Huntington Beach.

The day before we sent in the final proofs for printing, Ms. Sanford called me into her office. I sat down next to her desk, a little nervous. She called me into her office regularly, but it was usually so quick that there was no time for me to sit. I glanced over at her cluttered desk and noticed the proofs from the last couple of pages sitting on the top. Crap, I thought. It's going to backfire after all. I should have listened to Gavin.

"So," Ms. Sanford began. "I sent the last few pages into the printer's." She studied me, her eyes sharp. I nodded, unwilling to confess anything just yet. *"The printers were not happy with them. Do you know why?"* I shook my head again, my heart pounding in my chest. Had it somehow leaked to the printer? Was it illegal? Crap, crap, crap. Piper, I'm going to kill you, ran through my head over and over again.

"They looked at the pages and assumed that we had plagiarized another company's layout. Which, they so kindly reminded me, would void our contract with them. Not to mention the legal issues that would bring up."

I furrowed my brow, completely confused with this turn of events. "But we didn't steal anything," I interjected. "I did all the layout work!"

The first hint of a smile appeared on Ms. Sanford's face. "I know," she said. "That's what I told them. They didn't believe me. Then, I told them that you had also created all of the logos for the clubs. They didn't believe that either."

I couldn't understand why she was smiling. "But I did!" I said indignantly. "What are they going to do?" I could hear the quaver in my voice.

"They did their homework. They called me back a few minutes ago with the news that they couldn't find a source for the layout or the logos. And then they asked for that student's information. I told them that it was against school policy for me to give that out, and I asked why they wanted it."

XXX

"They want to hire me!" I yelled into the phone. I turned the car onto my street on my way home from school. I had just hung up with the printing company. They wanted my information to offer me a job. More like a summer internship, but it was a full time job with a better salary than I could ever get working at the community center. As soon as their rep hung up, I called Gavin. When he didn't pick up, I dialed James and caught him off guard with the good news.

"Who?" he asked, obviously bewildered. There had been little preamble before the announcement.

"Lifebook. They were so impressed by my design work that I did in the yearbook, they asked Ms. Sanford to put me in contact with them. And I just called. They want to interview me, but the woman I talked to sounded pretty convinced already. I've got an internship, and I haven't even gone to college yet!" I took a deep breath, trying to soak it all in.

"Sydney, that's amazing! We need to celebrate." This is why I called James. His excitement was obvious in his voice, even over the phone.

"Tonight. I'll call Piper, you call Sean and Gavin. I can't wait to tell my mom!" I shrieked, as I pulled into my driveway. "I'm home, I gotta go. I'll talk to you tonight!"

"Hopefully, my eardrums will have healed by then," James moaned.

"Ha, ha." I retorted. "Tonight."

"Tonight."

chapter fifteen

AUGUST 2017

What do you mean you have to work?" Gavin yelled. The five of us were finishing up dinner in Gavin's backyard. We were in the final planning stages of our Senior trip. Two weeks until departure. The yearbook scheme would cover two hotel rooms, minus the taxes, and we all took work off for one week. All of us but James. Only, he didn't tell anyone until today.

"I have to work, Gavin. I can't come." James got up and dumped the rest of his Cafe Rio in the garbage.

"We've been planning this for months! I can't believe they wouldn't give you the time off," Sean chimed in. James glanced at him, then back at the ground.

"I didn't ask for it off," he replied quietly.

"What?" exploded Gavin. "Are you serious? You're the one who suggested the beach in the first place."

Piper and I stayed quiet. I was disappointed that James wouldn't be coming, but vocalizing that now wouldn't help anyone.

I could see James's frustration building. "I need the money, Gavin. Not all of us have an unlimited supply of cash."

I raised my eyebrows in surprise. James did not come from a wealthy family. He had worked minimum wage all the way through high school and paid for his car entirely by himself. He had managed to swing a scholarship, but he would be paying for books and everything else out of his own pocket. Gavin, on the other hand, worked for his dad, and only when he felt like it. If he ran out of cash, all he had to do was ask his parents for it, and that was that. It had never been an issue before, at least as far as I knew.

"C'mon, James. It won't be the same without you," Sean jumped in before Gavin could respond. "You've got to be able to afford one week off." I could hear how disappointed he was that James wouldn't come.

"Hmm, let's see," James responded sarcastically. "Go to the beach for a week or eat for a month." He held up his hands as if he were weighing the options. "You know, I really like eating. I think I'm gonna stick with that one." He put his hand in his pocket and pulled out his keys. "I've got to go. I'll see you tomorrow." He headed around the house. I jumped up and followed him out.

"James," I called after him. He stopped and waited for me.

"Don't," he said brusquely when I reached him. I raised my eyebrows in indignation.

"Wasn't going to," I retorted in the same brusque tone. I softened my voice and spoke again. "I just wanted to tell you I'm sorry. And that we'll miss you. Sean's right. It won't be the same."

He gave me an odd look. "You'll miss me?" he asked, quietly. I stared at him in confusion.

"Of course we'll miss you. Why do you think Gavin and Sean are so upset?" He shook his head at me and fumbled with his keys. "Want me to bring you anything back?" I asked.

He looked up at me, an ironic smile on his face and shook his head.

"You're impossible, you know?" he chuckled. He unlocked the car door and got inside. "Hey," he said, leaning his head back out. "Bring me something awesome."

I smiled. "I promise." I watched him drive off, thinking about what he had said. Gavin came around a minute later.

"Well, did you change his mind?" he asked, taking my hand.

I shook my head. "Nope, but we're going to bring him the best souvenir we can find."

And we did. I made it my personal mission to make James feel like he had been there with us. I filled up a tiny jar with sand, and another one with shells, bought a stack of postcards and a T-shirt with a quote from *The Princess Bride* about Huntington. The rest of us had a fabulous week wandering around Southern California, laying out, shopping, eating out, and boogie boarding. The weather was perfect, the week was amazing, and the only thing missing was James.

The day after we got home, I called James and invited him over to dinner that night. "It's going to be like Christmas," I told him in an over-exaggerated voice. He laughed and promised to be there. I worked hard on dinner. We had eaten at a fantastic pizza place in Huntington Beach, and my goal was to recreate their BBQ Chicken Pizza, which was to die for. Once dinner was cleared away, I brought out the gifts. I gave him the stack of postcards and then the shells and sand, saving the T-shirt for last. I watched his face closely as he opened them, and I realized that even though he was the only one of us who hadn't spent a week in the California sun, his face was just as bronze as the rest of us. He smiled and thanked us politely for the jars, but when he opened the shirt, he burst out laughing.

"You found this there?" he asked. "You didn't order it online?"

I shrugged. "What can I say? It was meant to be," I replied with a smile.

"Wait," said Gavin, "what does it say?"

James held it up for everyone to see. It was a print that read: "Since the invention of the beach, there have been five beaches that were rated the most breathtaking, the most stunning. Huntington Beach left them all behind."

Piper read it aloud. "I guess I don't get it . . ." she said slowly.

"Seriously?" asked James with a laugh. "And how long have you known Sydney?"

"I don't either," said Gavin. I looked at him in surprise.

"It's from *The Princess Bride*!" I exclaimed in surprise.

"I don't remember Huntington Beach in the movie," Sean commented.

I shook my head. "It's not, of course. It's a play on words."

"What's the original?" Piper asked.

"'Since the invention of the kiss there have been five kisses that were rated the most passionate, the most pure,'" I recited.

"'This one left them all behind,'" James said, his eyes on me.

"Oh, at the end?" Gavin asked. I nodded. "Only you," he laughed.

James pushed his chair back and pulled me out of mine for a hug. "I love it. It's awesome," he murmured.

I pulled back and smiled at him. "Well, that's what I was going for."

"Now," announced Piper, "I think we need to show him the picture of Gavin's wipeout."

Gavin snorted. "Only if we show him the picture of you drooling in your sleep."

We moved to the living room while Sean hooked the camera up to the TV for a slideshow and Gavin and Piper continued to bicker.

"Hey," James said, coming to stand next to me behind the couch. "Yeah?"

"You didn't have to do all of that."

I smiled at him. "Yeah, I did." I elbowed his side. "But if you don't want it . . ." I teased.

He held up his hands in surrender. "I love it. You couldn't pay me to give it back."

"Good," I chuckled. "I almost couldn't believe it when I saw it."

James nodded. "It's perfect."

chapter sixteen

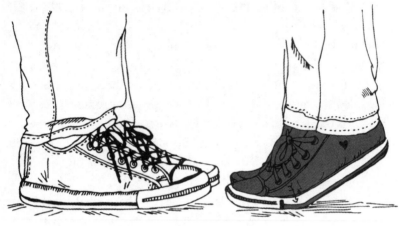

JUNE 2016

Our junior year was over and it was officially summer. The five of us drove up to Gavin's family cabin at Bear Lake. We spent the day on the water and after getting dinner, Gavin and I sat out on the back porch with raspberry shakes, gazing out over the lake.

"Did you see that?" I exclaimed, almost knocking Gavin's shake to the ground as I pointed to a distant spot on the horizon. "I think it was a bald eagle!" I stood and walked to the railing to get a better view. Gavin laughed at my excitement.

"It's just a bird," he teased. "We can go to the aviary if you really want to see eagles. And you even get to see those up close."

I glared at him. "This is totally different," I scolded. He shrugged.

"Whatever. Hey," he said, changing the subject. "Did I tell you about wakeboarding this morning?" I shook my head. "It was awesome. Sean kind of sucked, but I did a fantastic job." I nodded politely as he continued extolling his success. I let my attention wander back out to the water *as I half listened. I saw it again. An eagle, just close enough that I could make out the white head attached to a dark body. I watched, enchanted, as it dipped and swirled. The sun had just begun to set, highlighting the ripples in the water with a golden sparkle. I was mesmerized. I ignored the lake breeze whipping past me, making my eyes water.*

"Mmmhmm," I nodded to Gavin. I watched the eagle disappear into the distance, and when I was sure it was gone, I turned my full attention back to Gavin.

"And then he wiped out hard, but I stayed up the entire time and rode into the dock, almost." He turned to me, an expectant look on his face.

"Wow, Gavin," I replied, with as much excitement as I could muster. He smiled and began another story. I studied his face as he spoke. His gray eyes were highlighted by long dark lashes, despite his light hair. His lips were thin, but his round nose and cheekbones gave him a mischievous little boy look. I shook myself out of my reverie just in time to hear him ask if he could tell me something.

"Sure," I replied, shivering a bit. The shake, combined with the evening breeze was enough to give me the chills. Gavin noticed the shiver and chided me.

"I don't know why you never bring a jacket with you. You always end up being cold."

"Maybe it's because it's summer now, and let's be honest, a jacket wasn't high on the packing list." He smiled and took one of my hands in his.

"There's something that I have wanted to say to you for a while now, but I was just waiting for the perfect time. And I think this might be it. Sydney, I love you." He raised his eyes to mine, expecting a response. I leaned back in surprise, my eyes and mouth wide. My mind was racing. Before I even had time to process, his eyes drooped in disappointment and he dropped my hand.

"Gavin," I began, not knowing how this sentence would end. "I'm so, I mean I wasn't, I . . . I love you too," I burst out, honestly unsure whether I meant it or not.

"Really?" he exclaimed. His eyes lit up and he pulled me into a hug. "I was so nervous. I was almost sure you'd say it back, but there was a

chance. Whew!" he exclaimed, obviously thrilled. "Let's go tell everyone the good news!" He pulled me off the bench.

"Gavin, wait!" He looked back at me, confused by my tone. "Could we wait a little while?" His forehead creased in confusion.

"Why?" he asked, his voice full of disappointment. I tried to find an explainable reason.

"It's just such a big deal, Gavin. I mean to me it is, and I just want it to be mine for a little while, do you know what I mean?"

"Um, sure, Syd. I guess," his tone made it clear that he did not.

"It's just that it's special, Gavin. I just want to keep it special, just for while. Okay?" I pleaded, putting both of my hands into his. A small smile spread across his face and he squeezed my hands.

"Of course. I love you, Sydney Morris."

I smiled in relief. "I love you too, Gavin."

"Hey!" We both turned at the sound. James was running up from the shore, pointing. "I swear I just saw a bald eagle. Did you see it?"

chapter seventeen

AUGUST 2017

Our music tastes may have been very different, but that was one of my favorite things about Gavin. When I was in his car, we listened to whatever I wanted, and he didn't say a word. For the last month or so it had been my National Parks playlist over and over again. I discovered them early on in the summer, and fell head over heels. I'm pretty sure that Gavin appreciated them much more than the angsty girl rock that had been the norm to that point. And that might be the reason he bought tickets for their concert in Park City.

We drove up there early in the evening that night. As far as I knew, we were just going to dinner, and if I could talk Gavin into it, maybe some shopping. We did go to dinner first. It was delicious. Just as I was launching into my campaign to hit the outlets, we turned off the highway and into the Canyons Resort parking lot. I looked at Gavin with raised eyebrows.

"Was there something that you wanted to tell me?" I asked with a confused smile. Gavin smiled back.

"Nope. It's a surprise."

"Hmm," I wondered aloud. "Are we going skiing?" I teased.

"Ha, ha," Gavin responded sarcastically, as he pulled into a parking space. The parking lot was full and people in orange vests were directing traffic.

"A concert?" I asked. Gavin shrugged and turned the car off.

"You'll see," he said with a sly smile as we walked to the gondola. The ride up to the lodge was gorgeous. You could see across the Wasatch Valley and the sun was just beginning to set, casting a golden light over everything. It was beautiful. I squeezed Gavin's hand as we went up. He smiled, wrapped his arm around me, and planted a kiss on my cheek.

We stepped quickly out of the gondola as it reached the top and I saw the signs almost immediately.

Canyons Summer Concert Series
featuring The National Parks

I turned to Gavin with a huge smile on my face. "Seriously?" I exclaimed. "Do you have tickets?"

"Nah," he teased, "I thought we might just hike up the mountain and watch the concert from there." His smile gave him easily away.

"You are the best!" I cried. He put his arm around my shoulders and I nestled into him. "Thank you," I said, reaching up to kiss him lightly.

"C'mon," he replied. "Let's go find some seats."

We found our spot on the bleachers and waited for the concert to begin. It had been a long day at work and it was a relief to just sit next to Gavin and not have to think about anything. I watched as the sun began to disappear behind the nearest peak. It was the beginning of August and things were just starting to feel real. Only a few weeks of summer remained and there was so much to do before we left for college; it made the time seem even shorter. I leaned my head against Gavin's shoulder, just wanting to forget everything that was coming, and focus on the moment. Apparently though, that wasn't Gavin's plan.

"Can I ask you something?" he said hesitantly, taking my hand.

"Sure," I replied with a smile. He traced the palm of my hand lightly with his fingertips, keeping his eyes off of my face.

"What should we do in the fall?"

The question caught me off guard and I looked at him in confusion. "What?" I shifted to look at him more fully.

He furrowed his brow. "I already miss you, Sydney." He paused for a moment, then spoke again hesitantly. "I feel like you're already halfway gone."

I looked at him with eyes narrowed. "What do you mean?" I asked.

"Is this, well, is this the end? Do you . . . I mean, should we try to make it work long distance?"

"Oh, well, I hadn't really thought about it," I lied. I had thought about it. A lot actually. But mostly I tried not to. Neither option was terribly appealing to me.

"You haven't?" Gavin asked. I could hear the surprise and disappointment in his voice as he spoke.

"Well, a little." I relented. I paused and studied him for a moment. "What do you want to do?"

He sighed. "It really doesn't seem realistic to have a relationship when we're over a thousand miles apart."

"Okay," I said slowly, "well, then—"

He cut me off. "But I don't want to lose you. You might be the best thing to ever happen to me." His eyes locked on mine and I shut my mouth. I could feel a smile beginning around the corners of my lips.

"So, which one wins?" I asked.

"That's why I wanted to ask you. If I was going to make the call, I'm willing to try long distance. I love you, Sydney. I don't want to lose you," he repeated.

"Okay, then. It's settled," I said. "Long distance it is."

He searched my face. "It's going to be hard, Syd. And I'm only going to be home for Christmas and then not again until next summer. Are you sure you want to try it?"

I looked back at him with equal intensity. "I'm willing if you are," I said, squeezing his hand.

"Works for me," he answered with a smile. Before I could reply, the lights around the amphitheater went down and the opening act began their set. I gave him one last reassuring smile and nestled closer to him to enjoy the music.

XXX

Gavin's parents thought we were stupid, but Piper, Sean, James, and I had insisted on seeing him off at the airport. They couldn't understand why we couldn't just stop by the house before they left and call it good, particularly since that meant we all had to be there by 7:00 that morning. Actually, it had been Gavin who had pressed it. He never would have admitted it out loud, but I think he was terrified. Oh, he was thrilled that he had been accepted, but he was going alone and I think he needed those last few minutes with us to make getting on the plane a little easier to bear. We wanted to stand in the security line with him, but his parents strongly discouraged that, pointing out that the TSA would not appreciate teary goodbyes holding up the line.

We stood a ways back from security and went down our line. First Piper, then Sean, James, and then me. Gavin pulled me into a tight embrace. Gavin was a big guy and it was comfortable in his arms. I was enveloped by the smell of his cologne, and the thought that it would be months before I would be here again set the tears flowing. I didn't want to move, and when Gavin started to, I held on even tighter. He put his hand in my hair and his lips close to my ear.

"I do have a plane to catch, you know." His voice shook slightly, but I could hear the smile in it. I raised my face to his and he pressed his lips against mine, warm and comforting. Nearby, his dad cleared his throat loudly and we pulled apart.

"Love you," he said, as he pulled away.

"You too," I replied.

We watched him go through the security line and wave as he passed through the metal detectors. As we walked back to the cars, James put his arm around me.

"You okay?" I nodded numbly. "You want to ride back with me?"

I nodded again, grateful for his offer. I had ridden to the airport with Gavin and his parents, but the idea of getting back into that car without him was almost unbearable.

James flipped off the stereo as soon as he started the car, and I curled up in a ball on the front seat, watching James. He kept shooting glances at me, and occasionally reached over to rub my leg comfortingly. When we neared my exit, I spoke for the first time since we had gotten in the car.

"I don't want to go home yet."

James looked over at me. "Where do you want to go?" he asked.

"I don't care. I need," I paused, looking for the right word. "I need a distraction."

James drove past the exit. "Do you want to call Sean and Piper?"

"No," I answered quickly. I knew that I wouldn't be able to stand watching them hold hands and giggle together. James must have understood, because he simply nodded. After a few minutes, it became obvious that we were headed to the canyon. For the first time all morning, I relaxed and closed my eyes. When I opened them, we were at the top of Big Cottonwood Canyon, in the parking lot of the Silver Lake trail. I looked over at James. His head was back against the seat and his eyes were closed too. I wasn't sure if he was asleep, and I didn't want to wake him if he was. I glanced out the window. Even though it was late August, there were only a few cars in the parking lot. Out on the trail I could see a mom surrounded by toddlers and pushing a stroller. Her kids would run ahead of her, crouch down by the edge of the boardwalk, and point to the fascinating things that they could see there. They got so excited about whatever it was that they were seeing. I wished I remembered more what that was like.

The past week had been hard. My mom would drive me up to Boise in a few days. I had just said goodbye to Gavin, and as soon as I got home, I would have to go back to packing up my room. That was a soul-sucking task. I could only stand it for a couple hours at a time, then the reality of it all just got to be too much and I had to stop.

I had dreamt of this for the past two years. Living on my own, without the constant inconvenience of parental supervision. Moving past the trivialities of high school. New opportunities, new town, new friends. I should have been chomping at the bit to go. Six months ago, I was; but now, now all I felt was a vague sense of unease. I was jumping headfirst into the unknown. Alone. I didn't have a friend as a roommate—Piper would be going to school in California. I would be moving in with a perfect stranger and I was terrified. And my social life wasn't my only concern. I had pretty much breezed through high school, academically, but what if college was too much? What if I couldn't hack it? I watched those children until they disappeared from sight, jealous of their freedom. They had their whole childhood ahead of them. Mine would expire next week.

I don't know how long I sat in the car, staring out the window, but when I looked back at James, his eyes were open and on me. His mouth curved into a barely discernable smile.

"Stay here or walk?" he asked.

"Walk, I think." I pushed the door open and stretched. I had lost all sense of time, but the chill in the morning air made me think it was still pretty early. James and I walked halfway around the lake in silence until we found a tiny dock just below the trail.

"Let's sit," I suggested, pointing to the wooden benches. The water glittered in the sunlight, and a family of ducks swam in the distance. Towering pine trees surrounded the lake and the breeze rustled through them, making me feel like I was next to a waterfall. I breathed in the clean air and turned to James.

"How did you know to bring me here?" I asked.

He shrugged. "It wasn't hard. Whenever we are trying to find something to do, the first words out of your mouth are 'Let's go up the canyon.'"

I grinned sheepishly. "I guess you're right."

"I think if it were up to you, we would have spent every day this summer up here," he laughed.

"No," I disagreed. "The only reason I suggest it so often is because we never actually come up. Gavin hates it and Piper always has a better idea. And you know as well as I do that if Piper wants to do something, then that is what we will be doing."

James laughed again. "True," he agreed. He was quiet for a moment. "Is that why you didn't want to call them?" he asked softly.

I paused. "No." I thought about it for a few moments. "No, usually I don't mind when Piper rules the world. Honestly, it's better than sitting around for two hours saying, 'What do you want to do?' 'I don't know, what do you want to do?'" I shifted on the bench, leaning my back against James and stretching my legs out along the seat. "No, I didn't want to call them because they wouldn't want to be here. And I really didn't want to watch them make out all afternoon. Because you know that's what they're doing right now." I kicked my shoes off and let them fall to the floor of the dock.

James chuckled. We sat in silence again for a little while, staring out at the water. I loved breathing in the mountain air. It sounds crazy, but I always thought that I could tell how much cleaner it was up here, and it made my whole body feel lighter. It could have just been the altitude, but it was exactly what I needed.

"You awake?" James asked after a while.

"Mmmhmm," I answered, shifting my position a little.

"I thought I might have lost you again, you were so quiet." He paused. "Do you want to talk about it?"

I pulled myself out of my reverie. "About what? Gavin?"

"Yeah."

"Not really."

He squeezed my arm gently. "You okay?" he asked again, his voice concerned.

"Yeah. I just don't want to think about it. Because, if I don't think about it, I can just pretend that this is just another day. That no one else wanted to come up here with us and when we go back down, everything will be just the way it should be and no one will be leaving to go anywhere." I swiveled my head around to look at him. "Can we just do that?"

A sad smile played around his lips. "Sure. If I had known, I would have brought a tent."

I smiled and settled back in under his arm. We stayed there like that for hours, talking about everything and nothing until my stomach growled so loudly that James announced it was time to get some lunch.

chapter eighteen

MAY 2017

I don't think that I should go to Boise state," I announced. It had been a week since my Cal Arts rejection, and I had thought a lot about it. My mom needed me at home. Tyler needed me. Money was already tight and even with help from my dad, it was still a stretch. I could go to SLCC, or maybe even the University of Utah after Christmas. I didn't have to move away to get an education.

"Absolutely not," Mom replied loudly. She set down the newspaper. "You are not going to use me as an excuse to not go out and live your life."

"That's not it," I argued. "You need me. Whitney and I have to arrange our work schedules so someone will be here for Tyler. Whitney can't take it all on when I leave. She'll need help."

"Uh uh," Mom disagreed, shaking her head. "My schedule is going to get a lot more regular in a couple of months. By the time you leave, I should be working just about the same days every week. We'll work it out with a neighbor or a friend to pick up the slack when Whitney can't be here. You're going to Boise."

"Mom—" I tried again, but she held up her hands to quiet me.

"End of discussion," she said.

I sighed and stood up to leave the living room. "I still don't—" She shot me a look and I shut my mouth and escaped outside to the porch swing. I still thought she was wrong. I would be gone a week and the house would probably fall apart. It wasn't all that far. And I'm sure I could still get a great education closer. I rested my head on the back of the swing. Of course I wanted to go away to school. I was ready to be on my own, but not at the expense of my family. A car pulled up in front of the house and James got out.

"Hey," he called to me. "Are you ready to go?"

I stared at him blankly for a minute. "Go?" I repeated.

"We're meeting everybody for Sean's soccer game, remember? You wanted me to give you a ride?" He slid his keys into his pocket and approached the porch. "Did you still want to go?"

I shrugged. "Not really. But I promised Piper I would, so," I sighed and stood reluctantly.

"Everything okay?" he asked. I made a face at him.

"My mom is making me go to college."

James cocked his head at me, confused. "She's making you go to college," he repeated slowly. I nodded disconsolately. "I don't understand." James sat on the swing and pulled me down next to him. "Explain."

"I need to stay here. I shouldn't go away to school. They need me. Whitney and Tyler need me and my mom needs me. It's not fair of me to just take off to another state."

James narrowed his eyes. "It's not fair? Says you?"

"Yes, says me," I replied irritated.

"So, a week ago you were devastated because you weren't accepted to a school in California, but today you're upset because your mom is making you go to a school in Idaho."

"Yes," I replied petulantly, realizing how silly it sounded.

"You know your mom's right, right?" he said, biting back a smile.

"You are not helping," I shot back.

"Okay," he replied, getting to his feet. "But if you do not do this, Sydney, if you use this cop out to be safe, chances are you'll regret it for the rest of your life." He offered me a quick smile. "I'll tell Piper and Gavin you weren't feeling well." He took the porch steps lightly and was halfway across the yard before I called him back.

"Being right all the time must get really irritating after awhile," I yelled after him. He spun on his heel.

"Nope. Not really," he replied with a smile.

"Give me like five minutes, okay?"

"You got it."

We were only twenty minutes late to Sean's game. Piper and Gavin had saved us spots on the sparsely populated bleachers. Sean had been on the team all three years, but this was only the third game I had been to. It was also his last.

"Where have you been?" Gavin asked as I sat down next to him. I shook my head.

"I totally forgot about this. So James had to wait around for me while I got ready to go. Just a total brain fart."

Gavin nudged me with his shoulder. "You're allowed a few of those."

"Hopefully Sean didn't notice." I glanced out at the field.

"Honestly," James leaned over, "as long as Piper's here, I don't think he actually cares about anyone else." Gavin laughed and nodded. We turned our focus on the game, cheering occasionally when Sean made a great play. I caught sight of Beth from my art class in the stands and waved.

"That reminds me, did you get the invites for the senior art show?" I asked Gavin and Piper. It was an honor to be chosen for the senior class art show. Every student in an art class was offered the opportunity, if not requirement, to participate in the annual school art show, but only a select few seniors were given the chance to be featured. The art department went all out for it. Ms. Western cleared her entire classroom out for the event and then set it up as if it were a real art gallery. She made up beautiful invitations, got the cooking classes to make hors d'oeuvre for it and served sparkling cider in plastic champagne flutes. James and I were both going to be featured and Sean, Gavin, and Piper were on the invitation list.

79

"Got it yesterday," Piper announced.

"Last week," Gavin chimed in. "Do you have to stay all night?"

I cocked my head at him. "For the whole art show? That my artwork is being featured in? Yes. Yes I do have to stay the whole time." Gavin made a face and James laughed. "Sorry if that screws up your night," I added.

"It's fine," Gavin replied, obviously not catching the sarcasm. "We'll be there."

XXX

A week later James and I stood nervously in front of our chosen pieces. I had a ceramic vase on display as well as a sketch and a layout from the yearbook. James had chosen three photographs. Two were landscapes and one was a black and white photograph of his mother. It was beautiful. Guests began to trickle in, mainly family members who made bee-lines for their relatives. I smiled politely as people walked past glancing quickly at my pieces and then moving on to the next artist.

"You want a drink?" James appeared at my side with a flute of cider and handed it to me.

"Thanks," I replied, taking a sip. "No one from your family here either?"

He shook his head. "Not sure if they're coming," he replied quietly.

I turned to stare at him. "Not coming?" I repeated stupidly. "Of course they're coming. This is your senior show!"

He shrugged. "That doesn't mean a whole lot to my dad. My mom will probably show up at some point, though."

I shook my head in disbelief. "One day, when you are a rich and famous photographer, your dad is going to eat his words." James gave me a grateful smile, downed the rest of his cider, and returned to his post directly across the aisle from me. Several friends wandered through over the course of the evening. Whitney and Mom arrived about halfway through the evening.

"Sorry we're late," Mom apologized as she gave me a hug. "Whitney's volleyball practice went long." She focused on the vase behind me. "And

I decided not to bring Tyler. I didn't want to end up buying any broken pieces before going home tonight."

"I guess that's okay," I replied, only slightly disappointed. Tyler would have spent the entire time bored and loudly complaining anyway.

"Everything turned out really well," Mom praised. "You really are a talented artist."

"Thanks, Mom," I said quietly.

Whitney sighed loudly and Mom rolled her eyes. "Whitney thinks so too." I laughed at Whitney's consternation.

"I'm gonna look at James's stuff," Whitney muttered crossing the aisle. Mom turned around, realizing for the first time that James was right there.

"James," she said, "these are beautiful."

"Don't sound so surprised, Mom," I retorted.

"I'm not, I mean, I kind of am, but I shouldn't be." She glanced between the photos and James. "I mean, really, this is high quality work. I am really impressed."

"Thanks, Ms. Morris," he replied quietly. His cheeks were slightly darker than they had been a minute ago.

"I hope this will be more than a hobby for you," she encouraged, patting him lightly on the arm.

"I hope so too," he said with a smile. I walked through the rest of the show with Mom and Whitney, introducing them to several of my favorite artists and then walked them to the hall.

"I have to help clean up and then we'll probably go get ice cream or something," I informed Mom as they got ready to leave.

"Don't stay out too late. I know the year's almost over, but the key word is almost," *she reminded me pointedly.*

"Got it." I waved them off, and as I turned to go back into the room, I caught sight of Gavin, Piper, and Sean coming down the hall. They waved and sped up to greet me.

"What are you doing out here?" Piper asked.

"Just said goodbye to my mom. Come on, James is in here." They followed me back into the room and greeted James. We stood chatting for a few minutes and they did a cursory exam of our pieces.

"Everything is really good as usual, Syd," Gavin commented. "What time do you think you'll be done?"

"Um," I muttered, caught off guard, "I don't know. We have to help clean up." Gavin looked disappointed.

"Bummer," he sighed. "You guys ready to go?" he asked Sean and Piper.

"But you didn't walk around!" I exclaimed. "And there's sparkling cider."

Gavin shrugged. "We saw you and James. I'm good." He glanced at Sean and Piper. "Guys?"

"Yep," Sean agreed. "See you tomorrow," he called as they disappeared back through the door.

"At least they showed," James commented as he saw my expression.

"Yeah," I agreed half-heartedly. The rest of the evening dragged on and would have been unbearable without James. He was right about his parents: his mom showed up. She gave me a quick hug and praised my art, and then spent five minutes extolling the virtues of her son's talent to me.

"I'm pretty sure at least your mom knows how good you are," I commented after she left. He just shrugged with a smile. The room had mostly cleared out, but we weren't allowed to start cleaning up until the show had officially ended. I took the chance to study James's photos. The portrait of his mom was still my favorite, but on closer inspection, the landscapes grew on me. He had taken a panoramic shot of the valley on a clear day and it was beautiful. Streaks of white clouds broke through the graduated blue sky. The other was a shot from the Salt Flats.

"Hey!" I exclaimed in surprise. "Is that me?" I was so close to the photo that my nose was almost touching it. What I had originally thought was a landscape had a person standing, almost invisible, in the rays of orange light.

"That's you," he confirmed.

"I don't remember this shot," I mused, thinking back at the glance I had at the back of his camera.

"It's actually a compilation of two," he explained.

"It's really beautiful." I squeezed his arm lightly.

"*You generally have that effect on things,*" *he replied quietly. I glanced up in him in surprise.*

"*Okay, artists, the show is officially closed!*" *Ms. Western shut the door.* "*Come finish off these hors d'oeuvre, gather up your art, and get out of here!*"

chapter nineteen

AUGUST 2017

Over the next week, James and I spent a lot of time together. Piper and Sean were joined at the hip, and almost unbearable to be around, anticipating their upcoming separation. Which meant that James was the one I texted when I couldn't take another second of packing, and I was the one he called when he needed to go shopping for his textbooks. He was invaluable, and saying goodbye to him the night before I left was almost as hard as saying goodbye to Gavin.

Mom took me out for one last dinner, just me and her. She was as nervous as I was.

"You got shampoo and conditioner?"

"Yep." I ate a bite of salad.

"And tylenol? In case your cramps are bad?"

"Got it."

"Extra pencils?"

"Mom, we've gone over the list like three times."

"I know, but you have to remember your phone charger. I don't want to have to mail it to you."

"It's already in my bag," I reassured her. I glanced down at her plate. She had hardly eaten a thing. "Are you going to be okay?"

"Don't worry about me," she offered me a smile. "I've been doing this mom thing for a while now. I think I've gotten pretty good at it."

"I think so too," I agreed quietly. Mom looked down at her plate and stabbed a grape several times before looking back up at me. Her eyes were bright.

"What's your plan for tonight?"

"I'm going to Piper's when we're done. I won't be very long. Just to say goodbye to everyone." Mom nodded but didn't speak. "Is Whitney going to drive up with us tomorrow?" I asked.

Mom shrugged. "She keeps changing her mind. Tyler would rather die than make the drive, so he's spending the night at the Meriweathers'. I still can't get an answer out of Whitney, though. Have you talked to her about leaving?"

"Not really. I'm pretty sure she's been avoiding me for a few weeks."

Mom laughed. "Sounds about right. She'd rather do that than deal with the fact that she's going to miss her big sister."

"You really think so?" I asked

Mom laughed aloud. "Of course. Did you think she wouldn't miss you?"

"I don't know," I muttered. "She hasn't paid me much attention for a couple of years now. I don't know why she'd start now."

Mom cocked her head at me. "I think that you and Whitney need to spend more time together. I'll try and convince her to drive up with us tomorrow, but then your first visit home, you two need to, I don't know, go shopping or something together."

"Okay, Mom," I nodded, certain that Whitney would never agree to any of that. "If you say so."

"I do say so. And tonight? Don't stay too late. We need to get going early tomorrow."

"Got it."

XXX

The mood at Piper's was somber. Her car was packed, ready to leave for California the next morning too. We tried to joke around, tease each other like it was a normal night, but the jokes fell flat.

"I should probably go," I spoke up first. James and I had conspired to go home a little earlier than we normally would to give Sean and Piper their privacy.

"Me too." James stood. Piper hugged him first and then turned to me. This would be first time in our lives that we would go to school without each other.

"Call me when you get there?" I requested lamely.

"Okay, Mom," she laughed.

"Just call me, okay?" I hugged her tightly. She returned the grip and I could hear her sniffling, which set me off and soon we were weeping in each other's arms. Sean leaned over to James and muttered something and they both started to laugh. Piper and I pulled apart and glared at them and they just laughed harder.

"You're ruining this moment, you know?" Sean ducked his head contritely, but James's smile widened.

"Jerks," Piper muttered. She took my hand. "I will text you at least once a day. I promise."

I laughed. I already knew that wouldn't last. "Same."

I finished my tearful goodbye with Piper and walked out with James, still wiping the traces from my eyes. James didn't start school until Monday.

"You all packed?" he asked as we walked very slowly to my car, neither one of us really anxious to leave.

"I better be. If it's not in my bags now, it's not coming with me." I smiled sadly. "How about you?"

He shook his head. "I don't have to pack anything, remember?"

"No," I smiled, "I meant are you ready for school to start?"

He shrugged. "As I'll ever be, I guess."

We were both quiet for a few minutes, neither of us wanting to be the first to leave. I took a deep breath and steeled myself for yet another goodbye.

"Well," I began slowly, "I probably better get going." My voice cracked on the last few words and I cleared my throat, embarrassed.

He offered me a half smile and stepped forward to give me a hug. We had an awkward moment where neither one of us knew where to put our arms. He was so much taller than me that I could lean my head against his chest. He held me tighter than I expected, and for a moment, I could have sworn that he kissed the top of my head. I pulled back to tease him, but the serious look on his face stopped me.

"I'm gonna miss you, Syd," he said.

I gave him a small, sad smile. "I'll miss you too," I replied, my voice catching. He pulled me in for one last squeeze. "You'll text me?"

"Of course. You?"

"Absolutely." I didn't want to move. "Bye, James," I said, as I finally pulled away. The words felt insufficient, but I didn't know what else to do.

"Bye, Syd," he said, as I got in my car. He stayed there and watched me drive away until I couldn't see him any more.

chapter twenty

SEPTEMBER 2017

I went up to school without knowing a soul. There were only about four other people from my high school who went to Boise State, but none that I knew well enough, or wanted to know well enough, to room with. I felt a little bit like I had hit the roommate jackpot, though. Kelsey was fantastic, and only a little bit crazy. We quickly managed to work out a grocery system, a cleaning system, and a study system. Although Kelsey had a car, it happened to be a stick shift. A beautiful green Honda Accord with a manual transmission. Kelsey was really generous, giving rides or offering to let me borrow it when I needed it. For the first month of school, I conveniently only needed to go shopping at exactly the same time as she did, sparing myself the humiliation of admitting that I didn't have the first clue how to drive a stick.

There was only one person I knew, and trusted, who drove and owned a stick: James. So, when the chance popped up to catch a ride home for the weekend, I jumped at it, immediately texting James to make a space in his hectic freshman schedule to teach me.

He was only too happy to pick me up that Saturday morning, a perfect October day, take me to the nearest empty parking lot, the top level of a deserted parking garage, and watch me destroy his clutch.

His car was much older than Kelsey's, an old gray Volvo on its very last legs. James treated it like his baby, though. He bought it halfway through junior year and took amazing care of it. There was no eating in the car, and if you even so much as got close to scratching it, he would rip your head off.

He showed me where all the gears were, explained how the clutch worked, how I had to drive with both feet. And then he let me at it.

"Okay, so first gear is here, right?" I asked. He nodded as I shifted gears. "And one foot on the clutch and one on the gas," I muttered, more to myself than to him.

"And just ease on the gas. If you give it too much—"

The car lurched forward, made a horrible grinding noise, and died.

"—It'll kill it," he finished.

I turned to him with an apologetic grimace on my face. He gave me a patient smile. "It takes awhile to get the hang of it. Just barely press the gas pedal."

I nodded, concentrating. One foot on the clutch, one foot barely on the gas, ease into it, and we were moving, slowly, but moving.

"I did it!" I exclaimed, as loud and as excited as a little girl who has just ridden her bike for the first time. James laughed aloud.

"Now press a little harder on the gas."

"And the clutch?" I asked.

"Are you still on it? No, get off," he instructed quickly. "You only press the clutch when you switch gears."

I yanked my foot off. "Sorry." We drove in a circle going about five miles per hour.

"Do you think you might want to go any faster?" James asked with a hint of sarcasm in his voice.

"I kind of like this speed," I said, grinning at him playfully.

James laughed. I was a speed demon on the open road, and we both knew it.

"Because I'm fairly certain that the great state of Idaho will prefer you to go just a little bit faster, I'm going to teach you how to shift gears."

"Actually, this is the perfect speed to get stuck behind a tractor. So, I'm good," I reassured him. It didn't work. He raised his eyebrows at me expectantly. "If you insist." I took a hand off the wheel and put it on the stick.

"Put your foot back on the clutch, keep your other foot on the gas, and speed up a little bit and then shift to second gear."

I managed to take the car into second and then to third and got it up to thirty miles per hour, when James insisted that we try it from the beginning again, since that was the hardest part.

I slowed down, put it in first, and managed to turn it off without killing it. I even pulled the parking brake for good measure.

"Okay, try it again," James prodded. And that was where my luck ended. For the next thirty minutes I could not get the car to go. I killed it. Every. Single. Time. No matter how gently I eased off of the clutch, I couldn't move the car more than about five inches before it died with a horrible grinding sound. James winced every time the clutch protested, but was never anything but helpful and positive. I, on the other hand, was on the verge of tears by about the fifth time.

"I don't understand! I did it before! Why can't I make it work now? I'm doing exactly what you said!" I collapsed onto the steering wheel, banging my head in frustration and embarrassment.

James was quiet for a moment, letting me mope in peace. Then, softly, "You'll get it. Driving a stick is hard, but you'll get it."

I looked at him in disbelief. "This is not working. I'm a driving failure. I'm just doomed to walk to the grocery store for the rest of my college career."

I heard him sigh in exasperation. "Why don't we switch places? Maybe if you watch me do it a couple of times, it'll help." He opened his door and walked around the back of the car. I turned the key, pulled the parking brake and slid into the passenger seat. James sat down, turned the car back on, took off the brake and one hand went the steering wheel and the other to the gearshift. He stopped and looked down at the stick under his hand with a confused look on his face, and then he looked back up at me and started laughing. I stared at him, annoyed and confused.

"What?" I demanded irritably.

"It's in third," he gasped. "You've been trying to start it in third gear." He laughed even harder. "No wonder it wouldn't go."

I looked down at the stick in dismay. "Seriously?" I whimpered in frustration. "I'm never going to get this."

James tried to get his laughter under control, but it took a little while. I tried to see the humor, but I was so embarrassed and discouraged that it wasn't working.

"I'm sorry," he breathed, barely swallowing another peal of laughter. "I just couldn't figure out what was wrong with you." Out burst more hysterical laughter. I turned to him with a scowl and smacked his arm.

"You're a jerk," I muttered, but this time I couldn't hold back a smile.

"Wanna take a break?" James asked once his laughter was semi under control.

"I think we better. I would hate for you to fall tragically from this deserted rooftop," I glared at him, making the implication clear: stop laughing or die.

He bit his cheeks and slid out of the car. "C'mon," he called over his shoulder. I sat there for a moment, still pouting a little bit. He turned back to look at me and motioned me to join him. As I walked to him, he had an apologetic smile on his face. "You're not really mad at me, are you?"

I shook my head. "Only a little," I replied, unwilling to forgive completely.

We were on the top level of a nearby parking garage. I could see the mountains clearly. In the four weeks that I had been in Idaho, they had turned a brilliant shade of red. It was the one downside of living in Idaho: their mountains were not mountains. They barely deserved to be called hills.

"I really am sorry," James said, a smile hiding around the corners of his mouth.

"I'm not mad," I admitted reluctantly. "Just frustrated. And so, so glad that I didn't ask my roommate to teach me," I added as an afterthought.

"She probably wouldn't have laughed at you, though."

I could hear the penance in his voice and decided to throw him a bone. "Maybe, but I'm not sure I could trust her to keep such an incident to herself." I raised my eyebrows at him significantly. To my surprise, he started laughing again.

"Are you kidding me? This story is gonna be a classic!" He watched me as he said it, and I knew he was goading me, but I couldn't help it. I started punching him in the arm, the chest, wherever I could get a shot in. Before I knew it, however, he had flipped me around and had my arms pinned to my sides. His face was close to my ear.

"Kidding," he said. "No one will hear about this from me." He paused. "No one, but Gavin, Piper, and Sean."

I struggled to get out of his hold, but he tightened his grip around me. "Hey," I protested loudly. "Not fair."

"What's not fair?" he joked.

"You have the advantage of your ridiculously long arms. I have no such assets."

"You have plenty of other assets," he protested. I spun out of his grip quickly, surprising him into letting go, and when I reached out to smack him again, he put his arms up in self-defense.

"Truce," he called, backing away. "I won't tell anyone."

I glared at him again. "You better not." I flashed him a quick smile of forgiveness and turned back to the mountains. The morning air was cold and crisp and it made me want to go hiking, to spend the day up there. James came back to stand next to me, his gaze on the mountains as well. I wondered if there was already snow at the peak, and if the best of the leaves had already fallen.

"I miss this," I murmured.

"What?" James asked.

RIGHT NEXT TO ME

"This view." I nodded toward the canyon. "The mountains in Boise are different."

"Oh," he sounded disappointed. "We should practice some more," he said, shaking his head. "You still need to learn the difference between first and third."

"Ha, ha," I groaned as we headed back to the car.

"And, hey," said James, as we both climbed back in the car, "if you get it down by lunch, we might have time to get a hike in."

I smiled at his ability to read my mind. "Perfect."

chapter twenty-one

MARCH 2016

Are you up?

I grabbed my phone off my nightstand. It was James.

Yep. What's up?

I'm outside. Can you come
out?

I glanced at the clock. It was only 9:30.

Two minutes.

I pulled a sweatshirt on over my pajamas. It was starting to warm up, but the nights were still cold. I slid on my shoes and quietly slipped out the front door.

"Hey," I said. James was sitting on our porch swing. "What's going on?"

"I had to get out of my house for a little while. You want to go get ice cream or something?" he asked without really looking at me. I glanced down at my hashed hoodie and fleece pants.

"I'm probably not socially acceptable at the moment." I sat down on the porch swing next to him. "You okay?"

He shrugged. "It's my dad."

James had a difficult relationship with his dad. They saw the world entirely differently. James told me that once his dad had actually wondered aloud if James was really his son. He hadn't meant it to be cruel, but James was devastated.

"What happened?" I asked, covering his hand with mine. He glanced down at his lap and then out at the street.

"I had to get my registration paperwork for next year signed. I wanted my mom to do it, but she insisted we show my dad before I turned it in." He shook his head. "He totally overreacted. He wants me in Calculus next year, and he's telling me I have to drop Yearbook."

I sat back, disappointed. The plan was for us to be in Yearbook together. Along with Piper. It was the thing I was looking forward to most about my senior year. "He does?" I asked.

"I'm not going to," James shot back, his voice defensive. "It's the one chance I get at this stupid high school to take photos and have resources behind me that I don't have to pay for. I can't make it through Calculus. I barely scraped by through Pre-Calc this year and that's only because Gavin was at my house like twice a week helping me do it. Math isn't my thing, it's never been my thing, and he just doesn't get that. He knows how hard it was and he doesn't even care." James blew out his frustration and stood abruptly. "Let's go for a drive. I have to do something."

"You want me to drive?" I asked tentatively. He shook his head.

"I'm going out," I called inside so Mom knew where I was and then we were flying out of the neighborhood.

"Hey." I rested my hand on his shoulder. "You know there's a speed trap up here," I reminded him gently.

"I don't care. I don't care," he spat, but he eased up on the gas just a little. He pulled onto the closest freeway entrance and sped down the road. "I get it. He doesn't want me to be stuck in a dead end job that I hate like he is. But if I can't do it, I can't do it!" He hit the steering wheel and sped up. I listened to him rant for about twenty miles before he took a breath, and I took advantage.

"I know it sucks and he's annoying," I said. "But at least you have a dad that cares enough about you to drive you crazy."

He glanced at me with a look on his face like I'd punched him in the gut. "Sydney," he said slowly, "I didn't mean—"

"I know you didn't," I cut him off. "And I didn't say it to make you feel guilty. Just, I don't know. Recognize that you are lucky just to have him in your life."

He was quiet for several more miles. "Have you heard from him lately?" he asked hesitantly. I shifted in my seat, leaning my back against the door so I could look at James and drawing my knees up to my chest.

"He sent Tyler a birthday card. But other than that, not since Christmas." It was currently March. "When he came by in December, he told us he was engaged. I'm honestly not sure whether we'll be invited to the wedding or not."

"I'm sorry," he said.

I shrugged. "It is what it is," I replied bitterly. "And I honestly didn't say that to make you feel guilty, or to make this about me. I agree. Your dad doesn't get you. But he loves you and wants you to have a better life than he does."

"It's not a bad life," James pointed out. "I mean, yeah, things are tight, but there's always something to eat. Speaking of which, I'm starving. Want to go to McDonalds?"

I laughed. James was always hungry. "Yes. Let's go to McDonalds. You can buy me fries and a shake for dragging me out here in the middle of the night."

"It's not the middle of the night," he protested, exiting the freeway.

"Close enough." He did indeed buy me a chocolate shake and fries and then proceeded to steal half of said fries after he had eaten his burger and his own shake.

"Hey," I smacked his hand as he tried to take my last fry. *"There is a line."*

He shot me an innocent smile. *"You turned in your registration already?"*

I nodded. *"Last week. Yearbook, AP English, pottery, choir."*

"Sounds like a good year."

I shrugged. *"Should be. I have to take trig,"* I scowled.

"Well, Gavin makes a great math tutor."

I laughed. *"Between the two of us, I don't know how Gavin manages to get his own homework done."*

"I think Gavin's brain works faster than both of ours put together. Did he tell you he's planning on applying to Harvard?"

I nodded. *"And Yale, and Stanford, and Columbia."* I sighed. *"Pretty much anything a thousand miles away."*

James cocked his head at me. *"But you'll probably be in California or New York anyway,"* he encouraged. I smiled gratefully at him.

"Maybe," I replied. He reached out and covered my hand with his.

"Not maybe," he said. *"You will."*

chapter twenty-two

NOVEMBER 2017

I had never seen the Boise State campus empty as quickly as it did Thanksgiving weekend. Granted, I had only been a student for three months, but it was never less than bustling. I worked Tuesday night or I would have been long gone by Wednesday morning with everyone else. I was anxious to get home and see all my friends. Everyone would be home for the holiday. Well, except for Gavin.

Due to my car-less existence, my ride home was procured via the Boise State rideshare forum. Today's gem stumbled out of his apartment, half sober, handed me the keys and slumped into the passenger seat. The little red Mazda reeked of stale beer and something sweet.

A few miles from my mom's home in Sugarhouse, I began the attempt to wake up the still passed out Kyle. Poking and yelling had really no effect. Finally, after rolling down all the windows and blasting the stereo, he stirred.

"Hmmm? Where are we?" he mumbled.

"Salt Lake," I replied as I pulled off the freeway.

"Oh, right," he said, sitting up straighter and rubbing his eyes.

I pulled into my mom's driveway moments later, popped the trunk, and hopped out of the car without another word. The sight of my real home was a relief after the long drive. The maple tree in the front yard was almost bare, only a few golden leaves left clinging to the branches. The small, yellow house practically glowed in the late afternoon sun, made particularly beautiful by the deep blue sky behind it. I breathed in the fresh air and headed into the house, duffle bag in tow.

The front door was unlocked, and as I walked down the hallway into the warm kitchen, the smell of cinnamon was overwhelming. The sun was beginning to set, shining a golden light across the green and blue kitchen. The island was covered with flour and pie tins and the mixer was whirring in the corner. The apple peeler sat abandoned by the sink and my mom pulled her head out of the fridge with a stick of butter in hand when I came in.

"The prodigal daughter returns!" she announced as I dumped my bag and purse on an empty chair and came around the island to give her a hug. This was the first year in a long time she wouldn't have to work at all over Thanksgiving. The consequence of that, however, was that she would have to work on Christmas Day. She hugged me awkwardly, trying to keep her flour-covered hands from touching me. "How was the drive?" she asked, studying my face. I looked back at her, realizing how much I had missed her over the past few months. There was a smear of flour on her cheek and her long, red hair was falling out of the hastily constructed bun on the back of her head.

"Long," I responded, pulling a face. She leaned in to sniff my hair, wrinkled her nose in disgust, and pulled back to look at me.

"Maybe find a different ride back," she advised. I grabbed a strand of my auburn hair and smelled. Great. A subtle mixture of body odor and booze. I glanced down at my clothes, knowing that they too had suffered the same fate. A shower and fresh outfit would definitely be required before tonight. Mom glanced over at the newly created pile of luggage on the chair and raised her eyebrows in irritation.

"Dump all that in your room and come help me. No one makes pies like my Sydney!" she cried dramatically and turned back to the counter.

As I threw everything into the half empty, neglected-looking closet, I heard loud noises coming from the kitchen. I grabbed my chapstick off of the nightstand, slid it into my pocket, and headed back out to find Tyler just arriving home from school. "Sydney!" he cried as he saw me and threw his arms around my waist. I wondered if it was possible that he had grown since I was gone. Tyler was destined to be taller than I was: he already came up past my eyes. I ruffled his blond hair. He pulled away from me, a grimace on his face.

"You stink," he announced matter-of-factly. Mom stifled a laugh from her place by the sink. I glared at him.

"Gee, thanks." I replied, ironically. "How was school?"

He released me and grabbed a package of cookies out of the pantry.

"Boring. All we did was make stupid paper turkeys. But we got to eat popcorn," he shrugged, "so that was pretty cool."

I laughed at his attempt at being too cool to care. "Whatever," I teased. "You liked it and you know it."

He shrugged and wandered off to play video games.

"How's school?" Mom asked as I pulled up a stool at the counter and took over chopping the apples.

"Good," I nodded, concentrating on not chopping my fingers off. I paused and looked up at her. "It's hard, but the internship at Lifebook really helped. I think that if I had gone to school as soon as I graduated, I'd be totally lost."

She offered me a smile but didn't look up from the crust she was rolling. "You are so lucky that karma didn't come back to bite you on that one," she laughed. I looked at her in mock horror.

"You can't say that!" I protested. "You'll jinx it!" I looked back at Mom. "How about this?" I asked. "Someday, when I am a rich and famous graphic artist, I'll donate that money, plus interest, back to the school yearbook?" I raised my eyebrows, expectantly. "That way, I'm even with the universe, right?"

Mom just smiled and folded her piecrust. "If you say so, chick. Now, dump those apples in here, and let's get this in the oven."

Mom and I cranked out six pies that afternoon before I headed over to Piper's that night. As I pulled up to her house, I felt almost the same sense of home. I'd spent so much of my adolescence there. It felt strange now to have been gone for so long. I walked to the front door and noticed that the two chairs on the large front porch were no longer red. They had been painted a pale shade of green. Just another thing to add to the list of changes in the past few months.

The night started out with about eight of us in Piper's basement, catching up after the past few months of separation, swapping stories of dorky professors, stupid campus traditions, or ridiculous dorm rules. Piper brought down some popcorn along with a gigantic bowl of chocolate covered cinnamon bears, her favorite and mine. James raised his eyebrows when he saw it.

"I don't think you brought enough of those," he remarked sarcastically. I looked at him incredulously and grabbed myself a handful.

"One can never have too many chocolate covered cinnamon bears," I corrected him, popping one into my mouth with a smile.

"How dare you disrespect the bear?" Piper chided, eating one herself. He held up his hands in surrender. The bears disappeared quickly to no one's surprise.

After a few hours, most had gone home, leaving just the four of us: Sean, me, James, and Piper. Somehow the conversation that night turned away from college and back to high school. It was long past midnight and secrets began to trickle out. Most particularly, embarrassing crushes and embarrassing moments.

"You're kidding!" exclaimed Sean, "You bought him boxers?"

"Well, I was a very naive fourteen-year-old. And it was the only thing that I could find with a Snitch on it." I tried really hard to justify my purchase. "You would think that they would have Harry Potter T-shirts, but I couldn't find anything for anyone older than eight."

James just shook his head. "He was a Harry Potter freak. I should have known."

Sean looked at James slyly. "You're a Harry Potter freak," he said to James. Piper and I burst out laughing. James waved him off.

"That is beside the point," James brushed him off. "Sydney bought some guy a pair of underwear for Christmas."

"I was fourteen!" I cried, not doing a great job of holding back the gales of hysterical laughter. "Everyone had an embarrassing crush at fourteen!"

"Yeah, but not everyone buys their crush underwear," James quipped, barely getting the words out past his laughter. I scowled at him and suppressed a rogue giggle.

James and Sean were rolling on the floor. Piper was laughing, but she had been at the mall with me on the day of the infamous purchase, so this was not news to her.

"Back me up, Sean," I protested. "Everyone has a crush that they'd rather not admit."

Sean shrugged and shot a glance at Piper. "I've never been embarrassed by my crush," he replied, looking right at her. I rolled my eyes as obviously as I could.

Piper became thoughtful. "I don't think guys have embarrassing crushes," she mused. "Just ambitious ones."

I disagreed. "Their embarrassing crushes are the ones that they are serious about. Having a crush on some hot cheerleader isn't embarrassing. It's a badge of honor. Having a crush on one of their friends on the other hand . . ." I trailed off, allowing implication to finish the thought.

"Like us," Piper asserted. I snorted.

"Everybody has a crush on you, Piper," I quipped. "That's just a given."

James gave me a funny look. "Don't sell yourself short," he replied.

"What is that supposed to mean?" I laughed, playfully cuffing his shoulder. He narrowed his eyes at me in disbelief.

"Everyone had a crush on Sydney Morris at least once in their high school career."

I blushed, but tried to hide it. "That's not true. That's just silly."

Sean jumped in. "It's true. Everyone has liked you at least once."

"You guys are just being nice," I said, totally unconvinced. I looked back at James. "If everyone has liked me," I teased, "does that include you?"

James's face reddened. He ran his fingers through his hair nervously and looked away from me. I sat up straight, surprised by his response and moved closer to him, studying his face.

"You have?" I exclaimed. "Seriously? When?" I asked, curiosity drowning tact. He shrugged again, and still wouldn't look at me. Piper laughed.

"Oooh, James, you are so busted!" she snickered from the couch.

"When, James?" I prodded. "You're the one who brought it up, you have to tell me now."

He looked at me again, a small smile on his face. "I'm not going to tell you, Syd," he said quietly.

Sean, who was watching the whole awkward exchange closely, jumped in quickly, and tactfully changed the subject.

James was obviously relieved at the save and I left it alone for the time being, but my mind wouldn't. The fact that James wouldn't tell me when he liked me drove me crazier than the fact that he had liked me at all. I was determined to find out more.

XXX

The conversation slowly died out as our exhaustion set in. It was past one o'clock, and the rest of the house was still. Piper and Sean were intertwined on the couch, making up for their separation of the last three lonely months. I glanced at James as the other two made it physically impossible to make any further conversation.

"So, how's the business major?" I asked, skirting around the question that I really wanted an answer to.

He shrugged. "It could be worse. I actually only have one business class this semester. The rest are generals."

"Any photo classes?"

He shot me a pleading look. "Not tonight, Syd," he replied wearily.

I nodded. "You want to head out?"

He stood and pulled me to my feet.

"See you later," I called out as I left the room.

"I'll text you in the morning," Piper came up for air long enough to respond. I waved and James and me walked quietly out together.

It was extremely dark outside, the moon already gone. A nearby street light flickered, obviously on it's last leg, casting eerie shadows across the lawn. James walked me down the front path, all the way to my mom's car. When we reached it, James started to say goodnight, but I cut him off.

"So, uh, you going to tell me now?" I asked again, a playful smile on my face.

"What?" He feigned ignorance.

"You know I'm not going to give it up," I pressed. James just shook his head.

"You really don't need to know." The streetlight flickered off, leaving only the dim starlight to highlight the contours of his somber face.

I nodded solemnly. "I really do. Besides, you owe me one. You got to experience every embarrassing moment of my attempt to drive a stick shift."

James laughed. "If I remember correctly," he teased, "I was doing you a favor in the first place."

I shrugged with a grin and debated for a moment about giving in, but decided to try one last shot. "You know I'm going to keep bugging you," I added, "I can be pretty persuasive, you know." I cocked my head and offered him a coy smile, hoping to win him over. James gazed at me for a moment and then sighed and shook his head.

"You're impossible, you know," he said. I knew I had won.

"I know," I agreed, with a triumphant smile.

James looked up at the stars and took a breath before he started talking. "I liked you when we goofed off in Thompson's class and when you didn't get into Cal Arts. When you told me you wanted to get lost. I liked you the day you gave me that stupid T-shirt from California and when we went grocery shopping." His eyes shifted onto mine and stayed. " Happy now?"

It wasn't what I was expecting. I was frozen on the spot, in shock, unable to form coherent words. It took a few moments for my brain to kick in again.

"Why didn't you ever say anything?" I asked breathlessly.

James shrugged. "Fear. Stupidity. Gavin."

I took a shaky breath. "And now?" I whispered.

"Doesn't matter." He paused and shook his head, "I shouldn't have said anything. Do me a favor and don't mention it to Gavin, okay? Don't mention it to anyone." He turned to leave, but before he could make it very far, I reached out spontaneously and grabbed his hand, pulling him back.

"It does matter," I breathed. He turned back and gazed at me, and before I could comprehend what was happening, his lips were on mine and his arms were around me, pulling me closer. I retreated in surprise, but the car prevented me from going very far. I raised my hands to his shoulders, intending to push him away, but his lips persuaded me otherwise. I quickly got over the surprise and melted into him, wrapping my arms around his neck. With one hand in my hair and the other around my waist, he pressed me closer to him. I'm not sure how long that kiss lasted—it seemed like a wonderful year or possibly two—but James came to his senses first and pulled away. I sucked in the night air like a drowning victim. Everything around me was suddenly incredibly vivid. I could smell the damp leaves mingling with the musk of James's cologne. I put my hands on the car behind me, steadying myself. A frigid breeze blew past, pulling a shiver out of me that had lingered just below the surface.

"I'm sorry," he said, backing away from me. I shook my head.

"I, uh, no," I responded, hoarsely. I cleared my throat, trying to regain my composure. "Don't be sorry." I could feel my heart pounding in my chest and I leaned against the car for balance.

"You should get home," James murmured. He kept his eyes on the ground as he backed further away. I just nodded mutely and unlocked my car, lowering myself into the driver's seat. Before I shut the door, I looked back at James, now standing next to his car, watching me.

"Don't be sorry," I repeated, just loudly enough for him to hear. And then I pulled the car door closed and drove home in silence.

chapter twenty-three

NOVEMBER 2017

I lay awake in bed the next morning, staring at the ceiling. I slept fitfully, my mind bouncing back and forth from one disconcerting dream to the next. The past three months had been crazy enough. Moving out for the first time, attempting a long distance relationship, and now, this, whatever it was. I was barely able to keep my grades up high enough to hold on to my scholarship and I needed that scholarship. My part time job at Einstein's barely kept me from starvation, but there is no way it could cover any more of my tuition, which my parents currently split the cost of. I wrinkled my nose at the thought. It was in the divorce agreement that Dad would pay half. I didn't think he would have agreed to it if he hadn't been legally bound.

My phone beeped, startling me out of my reverie. A text. Immediately my heart began to pound and I could feel adrenaline start to flow. What if it was James? What would he say to me? What would I say to him? What if it's Gavin? A gaping hole opened in the pit of my stomach. Should I tell him? I hopped out of bed and grabbed the phone off my desk.

Happy Thanksgiving! I miss
you!

I collapsed back onto the bed in a surprising mix of disappointment and nausea. It was from Gavin. I crawled back under the covers and replied.

Miss you too! Can't wait for
Christmas. What are you
doing for dinner?

I tried to focus on Gavin, rather than on the fact that I had betrayed him. My shoulder demons were locked in a battle of wills, shouting down the better angels that tried to defend me.

It was James! He kissed you! Echoed the cry of the halo-adorned set.

But you liked it, came the taunting reply. *You kissed him back.*

My eyes wandered the room while I waited for Gavin's reply, lingering on the several framed photographs of us together that were hanging on my bedroom walls. There was one of us on the beach, our California senior trip, him in a wetsuit and me in a swimming suit, the ocean behind us and a surfboard in the sand next to us.

Went home for the weekend
with a friend to Hartford.

A photo from the concert that he had taken me to over the summer. The brightly lit stage was tiny in the background, scattered with indecipherable instruments. Our faces were pressed together in the dimly lit amphitheatre.

Glad you're not alone.

One of us at the airport, just before Gavin flew to Connecticut. His arm was around me, both of us with obviously manufactured smiles and red-rimmed eyes. His duffle bag lay at his feet and the security line was visible in the background.

Yeah. Better if you were my
company.

One from our high school graduation last spring, still clad in our huge graduation gowns, his blue, mine white, our arms wrapped around each other, his graduation cap forcing mine off of my head.

Agreed. Christmas!

One of us kissing.

Call you tonight?

My eyes stopped on the largest framed photo. It was one of the five of us. Piper was on Sean's back, piggyback style, looking as gorgeous as ever, her long dark hair framing either side of her face. I stood between James and Gavin, my hand in Gavin's, James's arm around my shoulder.

Sure.

Miss you. Love you.

You too.

I dropped the phone on my nightstand and stared at the last picture framed on my wall. A selfie of James and me, up close and personal, after a hike in Big Cottonwood. Both of us were sweaty and gross, wisps of my fiery hair flying in every direction, James's skin, darker than usual, juxtaposed with my pale complexion. And both of us with genuine happiness on our faces.

I rolled reluctantly out of bed and padded to the kitchen to help with Thanksgiving preparations. My mom could get a little crazy about Thanksgiving dinner. True, we had a big extended family, and since she wrangled the time off, most of them would spend the afternoon at our house. But my mom was incredibly particular. Along with the red hair, she inherited stubbornness, a hot temper, and irrepressible charm from her Irish grandmother. I got the hair, but luckily I inherited my father's single positive trait: a more even-tempered personality. Which made Mom and me a pretty good pair.

Mom taught me everything I knew about cooking, which was plenty. I could make lasagna at age twelve, and I had been making pie even longer than that. But I had a theory that she insisted on teaching me, rather than letting me figure it out on my own, so that I would do everything her way. I learned really early that if you were going to help in her kitchen, there was only one way to do it right. No exceptions.

Mom had spent all of her time off cooking to get ready for tonight. Last night, before heading to Piper's, we finished up the pies; no store bought in this house: pumpkin, apple, pear, peach, berry, lemon, chocolate, and even a key lime, ready and waiting for their time to shine. The bread for the stuffing was done; the veggies were washed and prepped for cooking. All that was left to do today was make the rolls, cook the turkey, cook the veggies, and make stuffing and potatoes. The last two were my job. Mine and Whitney's.

Whitney was never left out of the cooking lessons growing up, but there was a big difference between the two of us. I was good at cooking and I liked it. It came easily to me. Whit hated it. I don't think it was the cooking part so much as it was the being told exactly what to do part. While Whitney missed the red hair, she got Grandma's gorgeous blonde, she was cursed with the hot temper, and blessed with the charm. So even though in theory we shared the potato/stuffing responsibility, I had no reasonable expectation that I would receive any assistance from her.

Last Thanksgiving Mom had put us both in charge of the pies. It was a bad call that had turned into a sad, sad year for dessert. Whitney and I had been working on pies since we had woken up Thanksgiving morning, and Mom, for the most part, had trusted us enough to leave us alone. I made the pumpkin and the apple, and Whitney was in charge of the cream pies. Mom figured it would be harder for her to ruin the cream pies. She was so very wrong.

Whitney was stirring the mix for the chocolate cream pie. "Whitney, pour it slowly," Mom reminded over her shoulder, while Whitney poured the measured milk into the double boiler. "Slowly!" Mom snapped again, this time turning to watch as Whitney dumped the entire three cups of milk into the mixture.

"Whitney!" Mom screeched, "You're going to destroy it!" Mom hurried over and took Whitney's place at the stove, stirring frantically in hopes to save it.

Whitney glared back defiantly at Mom. "Fine," she snapped. "I don't need to help." She began to leave the room.

Mom laughed sarcastically. "You leave this kitchen, young lady, and we are going to have some major problems. Get back over here and stir this." Whitney rolled her eyes at Mom, which resulted in an unforgettable, drawn out yelling match. The pudding was forgotten, unstirred, burned, and ruined. Mom was furious; Whitney refused to clean up the burnt, sticky mess, and there were no cream pies for Thanksgiving. It was tragic.

Luckily, Mom had a long memory and the delicate pies were no longer assigned to Whitney's volatile care. Potatoes were much harder to ruin.

The kitchen was in even worse shape than it had been the night before. The finished pies were stacked on a rack in the corner, but the rest of counter was piled high with what looked like everything else. A huge bag of potatoes lay on the floor, next to a huge bag of sweet potatoes. Celery, lemons, apples, and asparagus were strewn on the counter and the mixer was kneading what looked like roll dough. I could already smell the turkey in the oven. Mom was still in her pajamas, covered by an apron. I wondered how long she had already been awake. She was washing her hands when I came in, and silently pointed to the bag of potatoes. I pulled out the peeler and the garbage can and got to work.

It's a very tedious job, peeling potatoes. Usually, when helping in the kitchen, I would talk to Mom, but Thanksgiving puts her into overdrive and it's really easy to say the wrong thing. Better to just avoid speaking altogether. I studied the patterned tile on the floor as my hands flew over the potatoes, tracing the lines with my eyes, desperate to shift my mind from flashes of the night before.

I finally finished peeling the last potato. My hand looked like The Claw, and didn't feel much better. I was stretching and moaning about it, eyeing the bag of sweet potatoes with dread, when Tyler walked into the kitchen carrying a basketball, followed closely by James.

"James is here," he announced unnecessarily, as he wandered through to the back yard, leaving James standing alone, an awkward smile on his face. He looked as though he was already dressed for his family's Thanksgiving dinner, in slacks and a button down shirt. His wavy hair was tamed with copious amounts of gel.

"Hey," I said a bit nervously. I glanced down, suddenly embarrassed by my dingy T-shirt and gray yoga pants. Mom said hello as well, but was too overwhelmed for her usual charismatic banter with my friends. I was grateful, because I wasn't sure how either one of us would stand up under it today. James scanned the kitchen, taking in the massive amount of food and our flour and potato covered visages.

"I'm sorry, I should've called. You guys look swamped." He kept his hands in his pockets and I could tell how uncomfortable he was.

I shook my head. "No, it's fine. Just let me wash my hands." I stretched my aching fingers under the warm water one last time, grateful for the excuse to stop peeling, dried my hands, and turned to face him.

"What's up?" I asked.

"I wanted to stop by and tell you Happy Thanksgiving," James tilted his head back toward the front door as he spoke, silently beckoning me to come outside with him. I gave him a nod and turned to Mom.

"I'll be right back," I appealed, setting the towel down on the cluttered counter. She gave me the look of death.

"Five minutes, Syd. These potatoes won't chop themselves."

I turned back to James, rolling my eyes. He grinned and I noticed, not for the first time, how nice his smile was. I grabbed a hoodie and slipped on my boots. We exited the house in silence and walked a ways down the road.

The sky was gray, but the air wasn't too cold. I looked over at James. He walked with his hands in his pockets, his eyes on his feet. I studied him for a moment, wondering what he was thinking. I had a momentary flash of his arms around me, pushing my back up against the car, but quickly tried to shake it off and regain my focus. I had to forcefully quiet the desire to throw my arms around James's neck and kiss him again. We both began talking at once.

"I'm sorry, Syd—"

"We shouldn't—"

We both broke off, glanced awkwardly at each other, and laughed.

"You first," I offered.

"No, you," he countered

I sighed. "Fine." I paused looking for the right words and failing miserably. "I have been thinking all night and I just don't know . . . You and I should . . . But then I remembered when we . . . And you, but that shouldn't . . . I mean, I, and, you know, Gavin . . . But . . ." I trailed off realizing nothing that I just said made any sense. "You first," I turned to face James, pleading. He offered me a small grin, which vanished as soon as he started speaking.

He opened and closed his mouth several times trying to find the right words. "I never should have said anything and I never . . ." He pursed his lips together into a straight line. "I'm sorry. If I could change it, I would."

"Oh," I breathed. Before I could get my bearings he continued.

"You are my best friend," he said, "and I don't want to mess that up. I was wrong. It was wrong." He trailed off a moment and his eyes focused on something in the distance behind me. He clenched his jaw and he continued. "And I respect Gavin too much. I just can't go behind his back like that. No matter what I . . ." He paused, and then said firmly, "We should just forget that it ever happened. It was a mistake and it can't happen again."

I stared at him blankly, a mess of guilt and anger and disappointment. I nodded slowly, trying to pretend not to be hurt. I began walking again when I couldn't speak, desperate for something to do. James followed and we walked a little ways further in silence. I tried to take a mental step back. He was right. In every logical, reasonable way, he was exactly right. Gavin was so good to me, and this was the worst kind of betrayal. Plus, James and I were so good as friends. I glanced over at him out of the corner of my eye. His head was down, his hands shoved deep into his pockets.

"I think we should tell Gavin," he said quickly without looking up. I stopped walking again, the gaping hole in my stomach yawning again. I didn't want to tell Gavin. I didn't want him to ask the questions that I couldn't answer. "He deserves to know, Sydney," he continued reluctantly.

I bit the insides of my cheeks and strode quickly away from him before he could see the clouds in my eyes. "Sydney," he called, jogging after me, wait.

"No," I spat.

"No, what?" he asked, bewildered.

"This would kill him, James," I replied in a low voice.

"I know." I could barely hear him.

"I don't know what he'll do," my voice cracked, but pushed past it angrily. "It'll change everything." James just nodded. "I mean it, James. Everything." I shook my head at him, furiously blinking back angry tears. "I can't believe you."

James cocked his head at me. "You're mad at me?" he asked stupidly.

"Of course I'm mad at you!" I shot back. "This changes everything. You ruined everything."

"Me? I ruined everything? You remember how it went, right? You pushed and pushed and pushed. So, if you're blaming someone for this it should be you."

"You didn't have to kiss me," I snapped back.

"So, we're not telling him, then?" he asked angrily. "It's not right, Sydney."

I laughed ironically. "Of course it's not right. Nothing about this is right."

"Well," he snapped back, "I guess I have nothing else to worry about." I pursed my lips, unwilling to feel guilty for the look of pain on his face, more satisfied that I was able to return the favor. "If that's how you feel, I guess I didn't need to come all the way over here," he responded, clenching his jaw.

"That's how I feel," I lied.

"Happy Thanksgiving," he said bitterly, and he turned on his heel and walked back toward the house where his car was parked. My anger began to wane almost immediately and I wanted to call out to him, call him back, but I was still too upset. I watched him wrench open the car door and speed off without looking back.

chapter twenty-four

April 2017

I applied to almost a dozen different schools, a few simply with a wish and a prayer. Carnegie-Mellon was my first choice, but there was almost no hope from the beginning. Not to mention the fact that it was on the other side of the country, and my mom was not made of money. Rhode Island School of Design and UCLA were also long shots, so when I got their rejection letters, I was a little disappointed, but nothing a bowl of ice cream couldn't fix. It was when the Cal Arts letter arrived that I really needed a friend.

I got home from school earlier than usual. There were no meetings, no events that I needed to be at that day. Tyler was at a friend's house and I didn't work until 6:00, so I came straight home with visions of a nap in my future. I grabbed the mail on my way in, and glanced through it as I walked down the hall. A return address from California Institute of the Arts stopped me dead. I stared at the envelope, my heart sinking at its thickness; or more particularly, the lack thereof. I moved numbly into the kitchen and dropped the pile of mail on the table. I slid my finger under the flap of the envelope, hoping that I was wrong, that this was some kind of preface to the information packet that was sure to follow. I held my breath as I unfolded the paper, but almost immediately my eyes flew to the words "regret to inform you . . ." I didn't bother reading the rest of the letter, but dropped it on the kitchen table with the rest of the mail. I stood alone in the quiet kitchen, letting the reality sink in. It was too much. I had to do something else. I pulled out my phone and called Gavin. He was notorious for leaving his phone on silent and walking away from it, but that didn't make it any less infuriating. Next on the list was James.

"You busy right now?" I asked as he picked up.

"Not really."

"I need to get out of here," I said, "Want to come get me?"

"I'll be there in ten," he replied, without asking for details. I wandered into the living room and sat on the couch staring into space until he arrived.

"What's up?" he asked with concern, as I slid into the passenger seat. I shrugged, not quite ready to talk about it. "Where do you want to go?" he followed.

I looked at him for a minute. "I don't know." I said slowly.

"Sydney, are you okay?" His concern was obviously growing. "Do you want to just go for a drive? We can talk?"

I nodded vaguely. He began driving west. I was quiet, but he started talking. He told me about his day, the stupid thing his math teacher had done this time, and his plans for the weekend. He even granted me control of the radio. We were almost to Tooele when he asked me again. "Are you okay? What happened?"

I took a deep breath and began. "I got the letter from Cal Arts."

He knew that Cal Arts was my dream. That I had every reasonable expectation to get in. I even tried to convince him to apply as well: they had an incredible photography program.

"And?" he prompted. I looked down at my lap and shook my head sadly.

He was quiet for a moment. I wondered briefly if I'd made a mistake in calling him. Maybe I should have just waited until Mom got home. She would have known what to say. I had just about decided to tell him to take me home, when I realized that we were slowing down. I looked up and saw that he had pulled off to the side of the road. He stopped the car, jumped out of his door and ran around to the other side, pulling my door open. He pulled me out of my seat and into his arms. I relaxed against him and the tears came then. The grief of my crushed dream was overwhelming, and I cried for a long time, all the while embarrassed by my outburst. James held me tightly and stroked my hair. When I finally calmed down, he took my shoulders and looked me in the face.

"I'm so sorry, Sydney. That sucks. They're idiots who don't know what they're missing." I smiled wearily at his valiant attempt. "I would usually say that this calls for ice cream, but I'm pretty sure that this is gonna take more than that," he added.

"Thanks, James," I said, hugging him again. He rested his head on top of mine.

"Anytime," he replied. We both turned back to the car as my phone began to ring. It was my mom. I sat down and answered.

"Where are you?" she asked. "I saw the letter on the table, but I couldn't find you anywhere. I was worried!"

"I'm fine, Mom. I called James. We're just driving around."

"Are you okay? I know how much Cal Arts meant to you," she said, her voice softening.

"I'll be fine, I just needed to get out. We won't be much longer. I have to work at 6:00 and I haven't eaten anything."

"Okay," she said, "Just be careful. I'll see you when you get here. Love you."

I dropped the phone back into my purse and looked back outside. James was standing by the trunk of the car, also on the phone. I stayed in the car and let him finish, thinking about plan B. Well, if you want to be technical about it, I guess it would be plan E. I sighed and leaned my head back against the seat. The disappointment was as painful as ever, but I was beginning to think of other options. There was always *the possibility of transfer. Or of graduate school. And maybe it would be better to go to school closer to home. I tried so hard to be positive.*

James slid back into the driver seat. "You look better," he commented.

"Apparently, all I needed was a good cry. That," I said reaching over and squeezing his hand, "and a friend." He squeezed back and shut his door. He pulled back out onto the highway.

"Hey," I said, "We need to head back. I have to work at 6:00."

"No you don't," he said simply, keeping his eyes on the road. I gave him a questioning look.

"Yes," I replied. "I do."

He shook his head again, a mischievous smile on his face. "Nope. You just called in sick."

I looked at him, eyebrows raised. "That's interesting. I don't remember calling."

"That's because your dad did. You are so sick, you couldn't even talk on the phone." His smiled widened.

"Really?" I asked. "And why would my dad do something like that?"

"Because. He's a pretty awesome dad."

"He's actually not," I replied. "Does my dad's voice sound anything like yours?"

James flashed me a goofy grin. "Yep, probably couldn't even tell us apart on the phone."

"What about you?" I asked "Don't you have to go in soon too?"

James shook his head solemnly. "There's something going around," he said, trying hard to keep a straight face. "I think I've come down with it too."

I laughed out loud. "So where are we going then?" I asked. The mischievous grin was back.

"You'll see." I texted my mom to let her know we'd be home later than expected.

We came to Tooele a few minutes later and James drove straight to the Cafe Rio. He ran in and came back out a few minutes later with a bag of heavenly smelling food. He carefully set it in the backseat and got back in the car.

"So, we going to eat that?" I asked, my stomach growling in anticipation.

"Not just yet," he answered and kept on driving.

It wasn't until I saw the almost seemingly expanse of the Salt Flats that I figured out where we were going. He found a place to park the car, and popped the trunk. I came around to find him pulling two camp chairs out of the back.

"Were you planning this?" I asked, confused. He shook his head.

"We got lucky. These are still in here from my brother's soccer game last week. Grab the food, will you?"

XXX

We sat quietly in the camping chairs looking out over the expanse. I had never seen anything quite like it. I had lived in Utah all of my life, but I'd never been out here before. It was almost like being on a lake, with islands jutting out of the sparkling water. Having grown up surrounded by mountains, I felt like I could see forever, and I finally understood the belief that if you reached the horizon, you might fall off. I fought the urge to try.

The sun began to set as we finished eating. I don't think James intended on staying so late, but both of us were mesmerized. The orange rays reflected off of the white sand and we were thrown into a golden world. Neither of us spoke as we watched the sun drop lower and lower, slowly disappearing over the edge. I've seen the sun set over the ocean, and that was incredible, but this was almost indescribable. I felt that if I ran fast enough, I could touch the sun before it disappeared.

James ran back to the car to pull his camera out of the trunk. I stayed where I was and I could hear him behind me, shutter clicking rapidly.

"Syd," he called a minute later. "Go stand over there." He pointed a ways off where our little picnic wouldn't be in the shot. I made a face at him.

"I'm a mess. You don't need a picture of me."

"No," he argued. "It won't be a close up or anything. Just your silhouette. Help me out," he begged, glancing again at the rapidly descending ball of fire. "Before it's gone," he pleaded.

Grudgingly, I pulled myself out of my chair and walked to where he was pointing.

"Face the sun," he called out. I obliged happily, not wanting to miss the show. I stood there for a few minutes, trying to fight off the chill that was creeping in with the fading sunlight.

"Turn sideways," came another shout.

"Seriously?" I yelled back.

"No one will even know it's you," he yelled. "Just do it."

"Fine," I grumbled as I turned as he asked. I kept my eyes on the sun until the edges disappeared and all that was left was a hazy glow on the horizon.

I turned back to James. "Done?" I queried.

"Done," he confirmed. By now the temperature drop was really noticeable and I clenched my jaw to keep my teeth from chattering.

"Can I see?" I asked as I approached. He beckoned me over and started flipping through pictures. He was right. With the sun backlighting me, you could hardly tell who I was.

"James," I breathed, "these are amazing." I knew that James was an aspiring photographer, but these were simply breathtaking. James brushed off my flattery and flipped the camera off. He noticed the chills that ran down my back and began to pack up the chairs.

"It's getting cold," he said. "We should get home."

chapter twenty-five

NOVEMBER 2017

Rather than head back to the house myself, I kept walking. I didn't think I could face my super stressed-out mother just yet. I was mad at myself for letting my temper get the best of me.

My phone beeped, making me jump. It was a text from Whitney.

Where are you? Dad just
called. He's coming over.

I scowled at my phone in surprise and dismay. Leave it to my dad to spring a visit on us at the worst possible moment. I slid my phone in my pocket and reluctantly began to trudge back to the house. Several cold drops of rain fell on my head and I shuddered.

I quickened my pace, hoping to make it home dry before the sky opened up. I didn't make it.

Tyler was bouncing around the living room by the time I made it home. "How'd you get all wet?" he yelled when he saw me. I pointed at the rain now pelting the window. "Oh." He glanced behind me and his face fell. "Did James go home?" I nodded as I tried to wring out my wet hair. "Darn," he said, sliding to the couch. "I wanted him to meet Dad."

That would explain the sudden burst of energy, I thought as I shut the door to my room behind me. I peeled off my wet clothes and towel dried my hair. Dad only showed up occasionally. He lived in Seattle; he had since about a year after the divorce. He was married again, but I still hadn't met his wife. He always came to us alone: we never went to him. When he was in town to see his parents, he would stop by. But he was only in town once or twice a year.

Tyler was only five when Dad moved out of the house. He could barely remember a time that my parents were married. He only knew the Dad that sent a birthday card and showed up on the occasional holiday with some piece of basketball paraphernalia for him. And Dad usually had a chapstick or lotion or something for me and Whitney. We tended to be much less excited to see him than Tyler.

To her credit, Mom was encouraging. Despite the way he treated her while they were together, she still wanted us to at least give him the time of day when he did show up. He was, after all, our father. So, we sat in the same room, phones in hand, and answered the few impersonal questions he had for us and waved happily goodbye when he left.

When I reemerged, mostly dry, Mom was yelling at Whitney to wipe off the counter while she and Tyler frantically straightened up the living room. "Good, Syd, help Whitney straighten things up in there." I nodded. Thanksgiving dinner plus a surprise visit from Dad was just about enough to send Mom over the edge. I quickly unloaded the dishwasher and filled it right back up again. Whitney was just finishing up the floor when the doorbell rang. Tyler ran toward it while the three of us straightened up and composed ourselves.

"Dad!" Tyler yelled as he threw the door open.

"Hey, Ty," came the soft drawling response. "You're bigger."

"Yep. I'm the best player on my Junior Jazz team this year," Tyler bragged proudly.

"That's great, bud." They appeared around the corner into the living room, Dad's arm draped around Tyler's shoulders. Dad scanned the room and took in the obvious food prep and stack of pies in the corner. "Wow, Andrea, it looks like you really outdid yourself this year."

Mom nodded politely and gestured toward the couch. "Have a seat, Cliff," she offered. Dad finally acknowledged Whitney and me still behind the counter. "Hey, girls," he waved. "Happy Thanksgiving."

"Happy Thanksgiving," we replied in monotone unison.

"How's college, Sydney?" he asked as he settled on the couch.

I shrugged. "Fine."

He nodded slowly. "How about you, Whitney? How's school?"

"Good," she replied shortly.

"Hey, Tyler," he said turning away from us. "Tell me about your basketball season so far." Tyler launched into a long play-by-play of the last game. Mom shot Whitney and me an irritated look. We were obviously not meeting her standards of politeness. But showing up on a whim twice a year barely warranted the civility that we were currently offering, so I didn't feel too bad about it. Whitney, however, tried a little harder and actually responded with a paragraph when asked about her sport of choice: soccer.

Almost half an hour to the minute Dad stood. "I really shouldn't keep you." He gestured back toward the cluttered countertop. "I know you have quite a bit to do still. It was good to catch up."

"Already?" Tyler whined.

"Sorry, buddy. Maybe next time I'm in town we can go do something." He said the same thing every time he came, but it never happened.

"Okay," Tyler agreed, still young enough to hope that this time it just might happen. Tyler hugged him tightly. Whitney and I didn't move.

"Well, bye, girls." He raised his hand in farewell and retreated toward the entryway.

"Hey, Cliff," Mom interjected. "Could I talk to you for a quick minute before you go?" I glanced at her quickly. She and Dad were pretty civil with each other, but her tone was funny. He must have noticed it too. He nodded and paused. "I'll walk you out," she offered. She followed him out of sight. Tyler disappeared to his room and Whitney and I returned to the kitchen. The potatoes were all peeled, now they just needed to be chopped. Whitney pulled out a knife with a sigh and I planned to join her until I heard Mom's voice rise in volume. Whitney and I both froze.

"There are three of them!" She wasn't yelling, but her voice carried clearly down the hallway. Dad's response was muffled, but with a quick glance at Whit, I moved closer to the doorway to hear.

"Andrea," his voice was soft and defensive. "It's in the contract."

"It is not!" Her voice was a little frantic, higher pitched than normal. "Clifford, putting Sydney through college does not negate your child support. The agreement was that you would pay half tuition for each child in addition to support for the others until Tyler is eighteen." My stomach dropped. Mom made decent money, but there was no way she could cover tuition and everything else without the child support.

"That is not what we agreed to." When he was mad, Dad's voice would go lower and lower until you almost couldn't hear it anymore.

"Please, please," she begged, suddenly conscious of her volume, "do not make me get lawyers involved. That is the last thing the either one of us needs right now."

"I need to go. Joanna is waiting for me." I heard the front door open.

"Clifford," Mom tried again.

"I guess we're calling the lawyers," I could hear him call through the open door. Suddenly the door slammed and I hurried around the counter, anxious to avoid suspicion. I felt sick as I picked up a bright orange sweet potato. Mom reappeared, her face cloudy. She stopped when she saw us chopping potatoes.

"How loud was that?" she asked.

"How loud was what?" Whitney attempted. Mom shook her head.

"You heard everything?" We both shrugged and kept our eyes down. Mom sat heavily in a kitchen chair.

"I could transfer next semester, Mom," I said tacitly. "I could go to SLCC. Live here."

She sighed and looked up at me. Her face was twisted. "Sydney—" she began. I cut her off.

"It wouldn't be a big deal. I mean, Boise is just Boise."

Mom shook her head. "We'll figure it out, okay? I don't want you to worry about it."

I offered her a small smile. "Okay. But, you know that I'm going to anyway, right?"

"At the very least, don't worry about it until after Christmas." She returned my smile and took a deep breath. "Okay. Potatoes. Stuffing. Gravy. And then I think we're done." She pushed herself out of the chair and acted as if nothing had changed in the last five minutes. "Now, where did I put my apron?"

I was distracted for the remainder of the day. Usually I love Thanksgiving dinner. We have a huge extended family and they all come to our house for Thanksgiving for one very good reason: my mother is an amazing cook. We fill up the table and all of the couches in the living room and everyone eats until they just can't eat any more. The kids run all over the house, the boys congregating in Tyler's room around the Xbox, and the adults stay in the living room chatting or playing card games for hours. I have a few cousins almost my age and we sit around and talk as well. I spent the evening being caught up on the latest in everyone's life and found myself hounded for details about school and my relationship with Gavin. I answered the best that I could, but was grateful when Mom called everyone back to the kitchen for pie. Thinking about Gavin right now just made me think about James and that made my head hurt.

As the evening wore on, I grew more and more agitated. All I wanted was to see James, to try and fix what was broken and figure out what to do now. When families began to trickle out, it got worse. My aunt was the last to go, taking her time, talking to my mom. I thought about just taking off, but I knew that would lead to awkward questions and I wasn't ready to answer them just yet. I tapped my fingers impatiently on the armrest of my chair as I attempted to read a book. Mom and Aunt Becca sat at the table still talking in hushed voices. Out of the corner of my eye I saw Becca glance over at me once or twice and pat Mom's hand consolingly.

Finally, I heard chairs scrape against the wooden floor as they stood up and my head whipped around to watch as Becca rounded up her children and headed out the door. She pulled me out of my chair before she left and wrapped me in a hug. "Your mom is lucky to have you, Syd," she murmured in my ear and squeezed me a little tighter.

As the door closed behind her; I jumped out of my chair and announced that I would be back before long. I pulled the keys off the hook and shrugged on a jacket. Mom looked at me curiously as I headed out the door, but didn't ask any questions.

It was dark when I pulled up in front of James's house. I glanced at the clock. 9:45. I hadn't even considered the time when I left. Now I was second-guessing myself. James had younger siblings. I couldn't just waltz up and ring the doorbell and risk waking them all. I fingered my phone, debating about calling. Would he even answer? I compromised with a text.

Are you home?

I sat in the dark car waiting for a response. I wondered if he would even answer my text at all. Maybe he was too mad at me.

Yes, why?

I jumped as my phone finally lit up with a reply and I quickly texted back.

Because I'm sitting outside your house wondering if it's too late to knock so that I can apologize.

Again, an answer was a long time coming. I rubbed my hands together to keep them warm and pulled my coat tighter around me. I sat quietly, staring at my phone, willing it to light up again. Just when I was about to give up hope and drive home, the porch light flickered on and the front door opened. James stepped out in a gray hoodie with a big red *U* emblazoned across the front and a pair of warm up pants. Before I could pull myself out of the car to greet him, he was sitting next to me in the passenger seat.

"Did I wake you?" I asked, looking at his unruly hair. I studied the lines of his face as he stared out the windshield. His long fingers tapped rhythmically on his knees, unable to keep still.

"No," he answered. "Just watching TV."

"Oh," I paused, trying to find the right words. I glanced down at my own hands, covered by the sleeves of my shirt, trying to stay warm. "James, I'm so sorry. I . . ." I trailed off, unsure again.

"Syd," James said, his voice softening, "Don't. It's my fault. You don't have anything to be sorry for. You were right to be mad at me. You're with Gavin."

I winced. "James. It's not that simple. I mean, you're right, I am with Gavin." His jaw tightened again. "But that's not what I'm sorry for." I shifted my gaze away from him, trying to make it easier. "Today, when you came over. I shouldn't have gotten upset. I shouldn't have gotten mad at you, I mean and I . . . just don't know what to do."

"You don't?" His voice was low.

I shook my head, keeping my eyes away from his. "My head is a mess." I paused, not quite sure how to explain. "It's just a big jumble and I don't know how to straighten it all out. It's too much to think about right now. And then today, my dad came over and I don't even know if I can go back to school after Christmas. It's too much. And then after he left, you were the one that I wanted to call and I couldn't and I hated that." James sat very still, his eyes staring out the windshield, refusing to look at me. His breathing was shallow.

"What are you saying, Sydney?" he asked, hoarsely

"I don't know." I moaned. "That's the problem. I just don't know."

We sat there silently in the dark, staring out at the dimly lit street. A cat ran across the road, it's shadow larger than life. A few cars drove by, and somewhere behind us a car alarm began to blare and then was quickly silenced. I ran my fingers around the steering wheel and folded them in my lap. But I couldn't hold them still, so I rubbed them back and forth on my jeans, trying to keep warm. After a few minutes, I felt James's hand cover mine. I looked over at him.

"I'm glad you came," he said, squeezing my hand as he spoke.

"I wanted to see you," I said. "I needed to see you. Especially with my dad and everything."

"Tell me."

I launched into the story, employing a few choice words to describe my father and his decision to stiff my mother. I began listing the alternatives that I had come up with for next semester, but he stopped me quickly.

"What about Cal Arts?" he asked, vocalizing the option that had been reluctantly crossed off my list. He shifted toward me in his seat, studying my face.

I looked at him, eyebrows raised. "Cal Arts?"

"Transferring? Next year? You can't transfer down to SLCC. Their graphic design program won't get you in."

"I know," I said sadly, "but I can't bankrupt my mom."

"One day at a time for now. But it'll work out," he reassured me gently.

I smiled at him gratefully. Our eyes locked and he reached out and brushed a strand of hair off of my cheek. His hand stayed gently on my face, cupping my cheek and pulling me closer to him until our faces were only inches apart. I closed my eyes, forgetting everything but the touch of his hand on my face and the sound of my heart pounding in my ears. I wanted nothing more than for him to kiss me again. Instead, my phone began to ring. The sudden noise made both of us jump back. It was Gavin's ringtone, and we both knew it. My eyes flew open. A hot wave of guilt came over me as I reached for the phone, but couldn't find it. It was somewhere lost in the darkness of the floor of the car. James pulled away from me and quickly opened his door.

"I should go," he muttered, climbing out. Abandoning my frantic search for the phone, I jumped out of the car and followed him up the walk.

"James, wait. Please. Wait!" I caught his arm. He stopped and looked at me. "That's it? We don't talk about it? We don't figure it out?"

He took a deep breath. "There's nothing to figure out, Sydney. Gavin loves you. He deserves better than this from me. From both of us." He paused, his eyes studying my face. "I've thought about it for a long time, Syd. It can't happen."

"James, please," I called after him, my voice betraying the shiver that was coursing through me.

"Go home, Sydney." It was firm, but not unkind.

"Can I see you tomorrow? Can we talk?"

"Sure. At Piper's party. Remember?" He had one hand on the doorknob.

I cursed Piper silently for the need to throw a party for every stupid thing. I didn't want to go. I didn't want to waste one of my five precious days with people I barely cared about.

"No, I mean before. The two of us. We could go hiking," I could hear how pathetic I sounded, but I didn't really care. He glanced back at me briefly and shook his head.

"I'll just see you at Piper's." He turned back toward the house.

"James."

He looked back at me one last time, his jaw clenched in determination, his features hard. "This can't happen, Sydney. Go call Gavin."

I stood and watched him walk into the house, slamming the door behind him. Finally, I turned back to the car, turned my phone off, and went home.

chapter twenty-six

SEPTEMBER 2015

Why?" Whitney shouted. "Why do I have to go?" She chucked a shoe across her room.

"Whitney, come on," Mom pleaded with her. "He's your dad and he wants to see you."

"Then he should act like my dad when I need him, rather than when he feels like it." She dropped to her bed next to me, her back to Mom. I kept quiet, despite my total agreement with Whitney's outburst. Mom sighed heavily.

"I know. And you're right. He should." Whitney's shoulders lost some of their fight. "But at the very least, go and get a free dinner out of him, okay? He owes you that much."

131

Whitney didn't turn. "He better not think that buying us dinner will make up for anything."

"I'm sure he doesn't," Mom soothed. "He just wants to take a step in that direction. I don't expect you to forgive him either. But it wouldn't hurt for you to move in that direction as well." Mom reached out and laid a hand on each of our shoulders. "I know that you two have taken on a lot of the burden since he left. Especially with me being in school and working. It means the world to me that you would step up like that. I know that he hurt you when he left; he hurt me too. But carrying this bitterness for the rest of your life will just make it heavier and heavier." Mom paused a moment and I glanced up at her. Her mouth was pursed as she tried to keep her emotions in check. "Going to dinner tonight might be the first step in letting that go." The three of us were quiet for a few moments. It had been a rough year since he'd left. Mom would finish nursing school in the spring and she could quit her second job as soon as she was hired as a nurse. We were all looking forward to that day.

"Fine," Whitney agreed. "But I'm eating fast. You better too." She looked pointedly at me.

"I'm right there with you," I agreed. Mom hugged both of us and left us to get ready.

Dad arrived to pick the three of us up half an hour later. Tyler chatted away the whole drive to the restaurant. Thank goodness for Tyler. He finally ran out of things to say when the waitress arrived to take our orders. Whitney and I both pulled out our phones and were texting instead of listening to Tyler. Dad had to say Whitney's name three times to get her attention.

"Whitney!" He reached across the table and covered the screen of her phone.

"What?" she asked irritably.

"How's school?" he asked slowly, daring her silently to return to her phone.

She took the challenge. "Fine," she replied shortly and began texting once again.

"You're a freshman this year, right? Whitney?"

"What?" She glanced up again.

"You're a freshman?"

132

"Next year," she corrected him, obviously offended that he couldn't keep that straight. Dad decided to cut his losses and turned to me.

"And you're a . . ." he trailed off, obviously not wanting to repeat the same mistake.

"Junior." I supplied.

He nodded. "That's a fun year. How is it going?"

"Fine." I was slightly kinder than Whitney about it, but neither one of us were willing to give him an inch. He doggedly kept on trying though.

"Have you done any more of your little art shows?" I clenched my jaw and nodded. "Your mom sent me a picture of the last one. It looked pretty professional." I simply nodded again, taking a sip of my water. The waitress appeared with our salads, saving us all from more conversation. Sadly, though, it didn't last.

Dad took one last shot at cracking Whitney. "So, Whitney, have you decided which classes you're going to be taking next year?"

"Nope," she replied shortly, not even bothering to take her eyes off of her phone. Dad slammed his fork onto the table.

"That's enough," he barked. People at surrounding tables glanced over in concern and curiosity. Whitney and I looked up at him in surprise.

"Geez, Dad, make a scene," Whitney muttered.

"I wouldn't have to if the two of you could just give me the time of day," he spat. "I'm not asking for much, here, girls. Just a chance to spend an evening with my three children."

I bit my tongue, wanting to avoid a full-blown tantrum here in the Olive Garden, but Whitney had no such qualms. "I'm sorry," she replied loudly. "Is it hard for you to have your family ignore you for an evening? I'm surprised you even noticed since you're so good at that."

"Whitney," he rebuked, his voice dangerously low, "that's enough."

"No," she disagreed, "I don't think so. Sydney, do you think that's enough?"

I shook my head. "I don't think that's even close to enough."

"Fine, girls, I understand that you're upset about the affair. But it has been a year, and I am trying here."

*I froze. "What did you just say?" I asked softly. Dad looked at me
warily.*

"What?" he asked stupidly.

"You had an affair?" Whitney asked hoarsely. Dad's eyes widened.

"You didn't know?"

*"Take me home, please." I put my napkin on the table and stood.
"Take me home right now."*

Whitney stood up next to me.

*"We are leaving." She pushed her chair away from the table and
I followed her silently outside. Dad and Tyler followed a few minutes
later.*

*"Girls," Dad pleaded. "I thought you knew. I'm so sorry. I really
thought that your mom told you." Neither of us spoke or even looked at
him. He unlocked the car and we all climbed inside, Tyler quietly complaining about missing out on ice cream. After an endless car ride home,
we finally pulled into Mom's driveway. Whitney and I were out of the
car before he put it into park.*

*"You're back sooner than I expected," Mom announced as we came
stomping into the kitchen. "What happened?" she asked as soon as she
saw our faces.*

*"Ask the adulterer," Whitney replied and disappeared into her room,
slamming her door behind her. Mom looked at me helplessly.*

*"Why didn't you tell me?" I asked. I had gotten bits and pieces out
the story over the course of the year, but that one major detail had never
been revealed.*

*"I didn't want you to think any less of him than you already did,"
she replied faintly. "I was trying to protect you. I didn't think he'd ever
admit it to you." She winced. "Is Ty okay?"*

*"I don't think he caught it," I shook my head. "He's pretty focused on
the ice cream he's missing out on."*

Mom sighed. "Are they both outside?"

I nodded. "I think so."

*"I'll go talk to them." She paused before disappearing down the hall-
way. "I'm so sorry, Sydney. I didn't mean for it to happen like this."*

"I know."

chapter twenty-seven

November 2017

I dreamt that night about Gavin. It was an unsettling dream with a lot of chasing and running. The colors were vivid and it seemed like I kept looking desperately for something that I couldn't find. I couldn't remember most of it when I woke up, only that I felt exhausted and sick and I finally ended up at work, slicing hundreds of bagels. Dozens of strangers stood around me watching as Gavin yelled horrible things at me because I gave him the wrong schmear and then James did too. I woke up sweating, my pulse racing. I layed in bed trying to shake off the unease of the dream and listened to the muffled sounds of Tyler watching cartoons down the hall. I wanted to rewind the weekend. Go back to Wednesday night and tell myself to shut up and leave well enough alone. Then I could be happy with my boyfriend, despite the three thousand miles distance. I could go back to school without a pit in my stomach. I took a deep breath and replayed happy memories of Gavin in my mind, trying to forget the drama of the last thirty-six hours.

I realized with a jolt that Gavin would be expecting a call from me, probably had been since last night when I never answered the phone. I leaned out of my bed and found my phone on my night-stand. It had been off since the night before. I worked up the courage and switched it on, wondering what would be waiting for me. I winced as the number of voicemails popped up. They were all from Gavin.

"Hey, Syd. I tried to wait until I thought all of your family would be gone, but maybe they're still there. Give me a call when you're done with dinner stuff. Love you."

"Syd, did you forget to plug your phone in again? It went straight to voicemail. Give me a call when you get it charged back up."

"Hey, I thought I would try one more time before I crash. Call me in the morning. Love you."

I set my phone down and collapsed back onto my bed. I really didn't want to talk to anyone right now. Everything was so murky. I felt like I was looking at my life through filthy windows and I couldn't see everything that I needed to see. It was becoming very apparent that I was more like my father than I wanted to be. Having a conversation with Gavin would require deciding whether to lie or confess. Neither was even slightly appealing.

But Gavin did deserve a phone call. I wouldn't want to tell him something like this over the phone anyway, I justified to myself as I picked my phone up and hit send. He answered almost immediately.

"Where've you been?" he asked, a hint of impatience in his voice.

"You were right," I lied quickly. "Forgot to plug it in again. Sorry." He laughed at me, forgiving me instantly. The pit in my stomach increased. "How was your Thanksgiving?" I asked, with slightly exaggerated excitement.

"It was fine. A lot different than my family's, but still fun. Cody's uncle got super drunk and then sang the entire soundtrack of

Hamilton, so at least the entertainment was good. And the food was great. How about you? How was your night?"

"Fine." I replied, trying to focus on dinner and family for a minute, rather than the way my night ended. "Mom was super stressed, as is standard. My dad came by and was a jerk. And of course the food was great. The family was a little obnoxious, but it was good to see them."

"Were they there forever last night?" he asked.

"What? Why?" I asked, caught off guard.

"I called around ten, but you didn't pick up. And your phone was still on." I tried to push away the memory of searching the floor of the car for the phone.

"Oh," I stammered, my guilt increasing. "Yeah, my one aunt stayed really late. So, yeah."

"So, have you seen anyone yet?" The question was innocent enough, but it caught me off guard.

"What? Who?" I knew I sounded like an idiot, but I felt so flustered that I couldn't help it.

"Piper, Sean, James, you know. You okay, Syd? You seem distracted." There was obvious concern in his voice.

"I'm fine," I answered quickly. "I . . . I think I'm coming down with something. My head's kind of fuzzy this morning. No, yeah, I saw everyone Wednesday night. We, um, hung out for a while at Piper's house."

"Did you have fun?"

"Um, yeah, you know. It was pretty low key. Piper's throwing a party tonight, so I'll see more people then." Gavin laughed.

"Classic Piper. I wish I was there to go with you," he added.

"Me too," I said. I meant it. "When do you get home?" I asked.

"My flight is on the 22nd, I think. In the morning."

"That's less than a month away! So, you'll be here soon!" I replied, trying to sound cheerful.

"Kind of. Hey, come get me at the airport. I'll send you all the details."

"Sure," I replied. The line got quiet. I realized that I was usually the conversationalist, but today I wasn't in the mood for talking.

Only when it was quiet long enough to start getting awkward did I decide to end it.

"Hey, so I guess I'll text you later, all right?"

"Sure," I could hear his disappointment that this hadn't been a better conversation. "Love you."

"You too," I replied and hung up.

I finally dragged myself out of my room to find Whitney in the kitchen, fully dressed after an early morning of Black Friday Shopping. It was kind of discouraging to pass a mirror and see myself in all my just-out-of-bed glory, red hair all over the place and bags under my eyes. Whitney looked up from her cereal as I entered.

"Well, you're looking good this morning," she laughed. I glared at her.

"Good morning to you too," I crabbed. I turned to the pantry to find something acceptable for breakfast. I slumped against the door-frame, sighing. The problem with leaving for college is that my mom stopped buying my favorite cereal and all I was left with was Tyler's Lucky Charms or Whitney's ninety-calorie cereals. I moaned at the choices and shot an annoyed glance at Whitney.

"Seriously, why can't you eat anything that doesn't taste like cardboard?" I whined, dropping my head onto my arms on the counter.

"It's just cereal, Syd. Not that big of a deal." I shook my shoulders with exaggerated mock sobs. "Seriously, Sydney, what is up with you?" she asked.

"I keep thinking about Dad and school."

"Yeah. He seriously sucks."

I sighed again, wondering if I was going to regret this. "And also James kissed me," I announced without prelude.

"What?" Whitney exclaimed, eyes wide. "When?"

"Wednesday." I put my head back down in my arms.

"What happened?" she asked, her cereal forgotten.

"It kind of came out that he likes me. And then as I was leaving, he kissed me." I winced in anticipation of her reaction.

"Did you kiss him back?" Her eyes were huge.

I shrugged. "Well, kind of." A smile appeared on her face.

"You did. You did! Are you guys together now?" I could hear her glee. If there was one thing Whitney can't get enough of, it's juicy bits of gossip like this. I looked up at her.

"No," I shook my head. "Of course not."

"Why?" she whined. "You should just dump Gavin and get it over with. James is better for you anyway." She went back to her cereal.

"Whitney!" I yelped. "We're together. And when you're committed to someone, you don't just drop them the second someone cute comes along. Just kissing him is bad enough."

Whitney cocked her head slightly. "You're not married, you know."

I raised my eyebrows. "What?"

"You're not married. You're not engaged. You're not Dad. This is different."

"It's not," I argued. "Gavin and I have been through a lot together and it's not right. It's just not." I stared down at the countertop, running my fingertips along the smooth surface. "He loves me."

"Right, whatever," scoffed Whitney. "You're committed to Gavin." She raised her voice, "Sydney, he lives in Connecticut! It's not going to work!" I sighed, regretting my decision to confide in Whitney.

"We'll be fine," I replied unconvincingly.

"Seriously, Syd, Gavin is an idiot to leave and think that nothing will happen." She laughed ironically. "Honestly, Gavin's just an idiot, period. Anyone that spends longer than thirty minutes with you and James knows there's something there."

"What?" I asked, annoyed. "What are you talking about?" Whitney rolled her eyes at me.

"Apparently, you're an idiot too. I take it back. You and Gavin are perfect for each other." The sarcasm poured off her tongue as she hopped off the stool and deposited her bowl in the sink. I watched her, letting her words sink in.

"Whitney," I said, hesitantly, as she left the kitchen. "I don't know what to do."

She turned back and stared at me hard. "You really are an idiot," she said, and left the room. I collapsed back onto the counter.

There were days, like today, that I wished that I were more like Whitney. I may have been older, but she was more, well, everything. She was prettier than I was, with her long blonde hair and fair skin. She was smarter than I was, with an analytical brain like my father's. Math, numbers, science, all of that was second nature to her. She was braver than I was. For her sixteenth birthday, she had somehow talked my mom into giving her permission to go bungee jumping. Honestly, I would die happy if I never, ever jumped off of a bridge, but that was all that she wanted. And she was more confident than I was. Things always seemed to come so easy to her; she always seemed to know what to do. And never in my life had I wished to know exactly what to do more than I did right now.

Three days ago, everything was straightforward. I would go to Boise unless Cal Arts accepted me as a transfer student. I would stay with Gavin, despite the distance. James was my best friend, a part time job was enough, and my dad was just somewhat of a deadbeat, rather than a downright jerk. Now everything was up in the air.

I snuck a piece of leftover key lime pie and wrapped myself in a blanket on the couch. I pulled my mom's computer onto my lap and started looking for job openings in Boise, and class options at Salt Lake Community College. The deeper I dove, the angrier I became. I was mad at Dad for being a tool. I was mad a James for screwing everything up. And I was mad at Gavin for leaving me.

After a long day of researching job options and student loans, trying not to think about James and moping, I made it to Piper's party, dreading the night ahead of me. I spent almost an hour carefully choosing my outfit, all of a sudden painfully concerned with how I looked for James. And then almost another hour debating whether or not to even go. I didn't want to be there. But it was Piper. Anyone else in the world and I would have stayed home. Instead, I pulled on my big girl pants and arrived to an overflowing house with bright lights and loud music.

Piper was the queen of parties. I take that back. Her mother was the queen of parties, making Piper the princess. Their home was old, historic almost, but when they bought it, they did a total overhaul. Piper's mom had parties all the time and she had specific requirements for her house: enough space for everyone, a fantastic sound system, and an almost commercial kitchen. It was always enough to draw out a major crowd.

It seemed like our entire senior class showed. I wandered through the front door, stopping occasionally to say hi and observe the niceties. My eyes scanned the room constantly looking for James and Piper. But mostly James. I found him before long in the kitchen, talking to a few people. He saw me, acknowledged my presence with a nod, and turned back to his conversation. I took the hint and kept moving, now on a mission to find Piper.

There were certain disadvantages to being the best friend of the most beautiful extrovert around. Piper's chestnut hair and charming personality cultivated friends without number, and admirers by the score. Sure, she had a boyfriend, for a year now, but that didn't mean that everyone she came in contact with didn't fall in love with her. So getting a few minutes alone with her at this party would be quite the feat.

I made my way through the house, plastering on a smile. I had almost given up when I finally found Piper and Sean in the backyard, snuggled under a blanket next to the fire pit. There were several outdoor heaters spread across the patio and it was almost as brightly lit as the kitchen was. I slid around the fire toward the couple and pulled an empty chair toward them. As soon as Piper saw my face, she knew something was up.

"Hey, Sean," she said sweetly. "Could you go find James? There's a bunch more firewood in the garage. We're getting low. Could you guys bring more out here?"

"Sure." Sean extracted himself, smiled a greeting at me, and disappeared into the house. Piper looked back at me, her face full of concern.

"What's wrong?" she asked, as I sat down next to her.

"Pretty much everything," I replied with an exaggerated sigh.

"What are you talking about?"

I began to explain. I told her about my dad's disruptive appearance yesterday and the revelation that came with it. I quickly ran over my options for next semester.

"That sucks, Syd, I'm really sorry."

"Oh," I interjected. "There's more."

She was there for the catalyst conversation Wednesday night, so I didn't need to do more than remind her of it. I explained what happened when James walked me to my car, how he had come to see me the next day and how I yelled at him. I told her I had gone to his house last night to try and make things right, but all that I had done was make it worse. I turned my eyes away from the fire and onto her face. Her eyes were wide and her mouth was gaping.

"Any advice you might have would be appreciated," I finished, turning back to the fire. It was silent for a long time.

"Are you freaking kidding me?" she said slowly. I let out a humorless snort of laughter.

"I wish."

"Sydney—" she began, but stopped abruptly as Sean and James came around the corner, arms loaded down with firewood. Piper and I watched in silence as they piled the wood next to the pit. Sean sat back on the other side of Piper and James turned to go back into the house. Sean called him back.

"Where are you going? Stay out here with us."

James glanced at me briefly. I kept my face noncommittal. He looked at Sean, "Nah, it's too cold out here. You guys are crazy." He turned to go again, but Sean wouldn't let him.

"Seriously, we get to see these girls for five days after being gone for three months and you can't stand a little cold?"

I kept my eyes on the fire, unwilling to participate.

"Fine," James huffed and sat down on the other side of Sean. I glanced at him as he sat down. He looked particularly nice tonight, in dark wash jeans and a sweater. Sean glanced between James and me, his eyebrows raised.

"Everything okay between you guys?" he asked, warily.

"Fine," James and I responded in unison, a little too quickly.

"Okay," murmured Sean, obviously not convinced.

"So," said Piper, a little too cheerfully, "What do you guys want to do tomorrow?" James and I were both silent, staring into the depths of the fire.

"Hey," Sean interjected, "my uncle offered to let us use his cabin again. There's plenty of snow in Park City, we should go sledding!" Sean looked around at the rest of us like he was expecting a cheer or something. I kept my eyes on the fire.

"That would be so much fun!" Piper agreed. "Sydney, you in?"

"Sure." I responded dully.

Sean turned to James. "What about you?"

James hesitated. "I don't know. I really need to work." James kept his gaze off the rest of us as he spoke.

"This is one day, not an entire week. Plus," Sean's voice rose over James's objections, "I know for a fact that you took an extra shift today."

James closed his mouth and turned back to the fire, rolling his eyes. "Fine," his voice was hollow.

"Seriously, man, what is up with you tonight?" Sean asked, his annoyance obvious.

"Nothing. I'm fine. But you know what? I think I'll head out." He rose without looking at any of us. "See you tomorrow."

As he walked back toward the house Sean called out, "Hey, could you drive tomorrow? We'll all help with gas."

"Whatever," James called back without turning his head. The door slammed shut behind him. Sean looked at Piper and me.

"Do you guys know what his deal is?"

"Nope," we both replied, resolutely keeping our eyes down. Sean didn't notice.

"Weird."

chapter twenty-eight

AUGUST 2014

On our first real date Gavin took me to a little Italian place that I had never been to before, and it was fantastic. Over dinner he told me all about his family. He had two older sisters, one already married with a kid, the other in college, and a younger brother, about a year younger than Whitney.

"Do you see your sisters very often?" I asked, pushing the last few pieces of ravioli around on my plate. Gavin shrugged.

"Janie lives in New Mexico, so we really only get to see them on holidays. Tori goes to Stanford, but she's home for the summer. But I don't really see her," he mused with a grin, "which isn't awful. We don't get along all that well."

"Why don't you see her?" I asked as I stirred the ice in my soda with the straw.

"She works like a maniac over the summer. She's got a pretty good job too, makes enough so that she doesn't have to work while she's going to school." I nodded slowly, gazing at his eyes. They were the most wonderful gray. I had never thought much of gray eyes, but Gavin's eyes changed my mind about that.

Gavin noticed my lack of enthusiasm over my plate. "You don't like it?" He sounded disappointed. His plate had been clean for a while. I shook my head vigorously.

"No, I love it, I'm just stuffed," I responded truthfully. The amazing bread that they kept dropping off had filled me to capacity, and while the ravioli was delicious, I thought that if I took another bite, I just might die.

"The bread?" Gavin asked sagely. I nodded sheepishly. "I did that the first time I came here too. It's so good, it's hard to stop." I nodded again. Gavin waved our server over, got a couple of boxes for our food, and paid the check. "Let's go," he said, pulling me out of my chair.

"Where to?" I asked, my hand remaining happily in his as we exited the restaurant. It was a warm summer night, the sky still mostly light, but the shadows were quickly lengthening.

"Well, I was going to suggest dessert, but now I'm thinking that's not the best course of action." Gavin laughed.

I clutched my stomach and nodded. "Maybe not just yet," I agreed.

He glanced around, taking in the shops surrounding us. "Hey," he said slowly, "I need to make a quick phone call. Do you want to window shop or something for a minute while I do that?"

"Sure," I answered hesitantly. "I'll just be in there." I pointed to The Body Shop and he nodded, pulling out his phone. I walked into the wonderful smelling store, a little confused. Who did he have to call in private? Was he just a jerk, and this was the first time I noticed it? By the time he found me, I was a little disgruntled and on the verge of asking him to just take me home. He smiled as he pulled me away from the body butter display and out of the shop.

"So, what's the plan?" I asked impatiently, as he pulled me toward the car. He glanced back at me with a grin.

"It's a surprise." He started the car and pulled onto the freeway, trying to keep the conversation going as smoothly as it had been at dinner. I was still a little put out, and my answers may have been a bit shorter than was polite. We finally pulled up in front of Gavin's house. I instinctively headed for the front door, but he called me back.

"Let's go around back, Syd," he called, beckoning me to a side gate.

I switched direction and followed him around the side of the house. And stopped. A white sheet was hung across the back fence and a projector set up on a table in the middle of the yard. Between the table and the fence was a pile of blankets and pillows, drinks, and a massive bowl of popcorn. I caught my breath and turned to Gavin with a smile.

"Much better than a theatre," he said, pulling me to the blankets. He switched on the projector and settled down next to me, pulling the bowl of popcorn into his lap.

I glanced at him with narrowed eyes. "Is this the phone call you made?" I asked curiously. He shrugged.

"We were going to be too early," he admitted. "Brandon set it up for me."

"Your brother?" I asked. Gavin nodded. "I like your brother," I approved with a smile. The main titles of the movie popped up as a familiar theme filled the air. It was The Princess Bride. I gasped. "How did you know?" I asked, nestling closer to him. He smiled as he wrapped an arm around me.

"I did my homework," he replied, finishing the thought with a kiss on the cheek. We'd spent the rest of the evening snuggled together under the blankets and the stars with my favorite movie.

chapter twenty-nine

November 2017

It became pretty evident the next morning why Sean wanted James to drive. Sean and Piper spent the hour-long car ride making out in the back seat. James blasted the stereo, trying to drown them out, but it was a long, awkward ride. They came to pick me up last, and Sean and Piper were already at it when I slid into the car. I glanced back at them in disgust and then back to James. His face mirrored mine.

"How's it going, James?" I asked, my voice louder than necessary in an attempt to get them to come up for air. It didn't work. James made an indecipherable noise.

"Great," he responded sarcastically. "Just great." As we drove onto the on ramp I glanced in the back seat again.

"Do you have a blanket or something that we can just throw over the top of them?" I asked.

"Just don't turn around," giggled Piper from the back seat. I rolled my eyes and tried to keep them front and center.

With things being the way they were, I didn't even attempt to mess with the radio, knowing that if I did, the floodgates might simply explode. Instead, I tried to make conversation, but James refused to give me more than one word answers every time I tried to talk to him, so I gave up pretty quickly. Instead, I stared out the window, letting my mind roam. It bounced from learning to drive a stick shift to wondering if there were any design companies hiring in Boise and back to Mr. Thompson's class in the tenth grade. I had an image in my mind of an irate teacher trying to figure out who had screwed with the classroom clock. I laughed out loud as I remembered. James glanced over at me.

"You okay?" he asked sarcastically.

"Fine, just remembered something . . . funny," I replied, turning back to the window. "You remember Thompson's class?" I asked on a whim.

"Sure."

"Just thinking about the stupid stuff we did in there. Do you remember the day that you set his clock forward fifteen minutes?"

James face cracked for the first time all morning. "He got totally flustered when the bell didn't ring," he reminisced. "And it only worked because he is the one human being on the planet without a cell phone."

"And we spent those last fifteen minutes doing nothing, while he went down to the office to make sure the bells were still working," I concluded. "Did you ever get caught for that?"

James shook his head. "I'm pretty sure he knew it was me, but there was nothing he could do about it. No one saw me do it." He smiled at the memory.

"Or the day we did *The Odyssey* report? I gotta tell you, you pulled off the toga quite nicely," I teased, smiling at him. I could see his smile widen. "But you know," I joked, "I still think you should have let me be Penelope instead of Athena. I could have woven a tapestry!" I laughed, remembering Mr. Thompson's face when we had shown up in costume.

James snorted softly. "You're impossible," he said, his voice low.

"I know."

We pulled up to the cabin about twenty minutes later. Sean was right; there was plenty of snow for sledding. The rain from yesterday in the valley must have been snow up here, because there was beautiful white powder in every direction. At least a foot of it perched on the steep red-shingled roof, threatening to slide to the ground at any moment. The cabin looked like a fairy tale, with blue shutters and gables, sparkling underneath the heavy snow.

We quickly unloaded our sledding gear from the trunk as Sean unlocked the front door. I had been here before, but that didn't prevent me from being amazed all over again as I stepped inside. The word *cabin* did not do it justice. Sure, it was in the mountains, but that is right about where the definition stopped being accurate. Sean's uncle owned some kind of successful software company in California, but he was only here a few times a year. His cabin was really a six-bedroom house; complete with four flat-screen TVs, a hot tub, multiple fireplaces, and floor to ceiling windows on the main floor overlooking an entire mountain. Honestly, once we were inside, I didn't even really want to go sledding. I just wanted to light a fire and curl up on the couch with a blanket and a book. I walked to the windows, gazing down on the snow-covered hills below. The view was breathtaking, an endless expanse of perfect snow. It seemed such a shame to ruin it with something as trivial as sledding. I turned around to find everyone pulling on their boots and snow pants. I sighed in resignation and pulled my own boots on.

We all headed outside looking like Randy from *A Christmas Story*. The sun reflecting off the snow blinded me and I realized that I left my sunglasses inside.

"Be right back," I called, as I ducked back inside. I rummaged through my purse, positive that they were in there somewhere. *I had them in the car*, I thought, *What did I do with them?* I began pulling everything out of my purse to find them. They were tucked behind my wallet at the very bottom. I slid them on and stood, watching my friends through the wall of windows. It seemed Piper and Sean had gotten most of their PDA out of their systems in the car and were goofing off. I slid into a chair and watched them. *I should just stay in here*, I thought. *It would be less awkward for everyone.*

"Hey, are you coming?" Piper yelled, sticking her head back in the door to urge me on. I sat back on my heels and looked at her plaintively. She shut the door behind her, and came closer.

"What's up?" she asked impatiently. I shot her a glare and threw my hands in the air.

"Managed to detach Sean from your hip, I see," I quipped. She glared right back.

"Honestly, Syd, that was a defense mechanism. Neither of us wanted to deal with your awkwardness."

I raised my eyebrows at her. "Right, so, you decided to take things to an entirely new level of awkwardness, instead. Great plan."

She shrugged. "Hey, it wasn't awkward for me," Piper said with a suggestive smile. I rolled my eyes at her and pushed myself reluctantly out of the chair.

"Sydney," she called as I reached for the doorknob. I turned around, still annoyed at her.

"What?"

"It'll get better," she soothed apologetically. I cocked an eyebrow skeptically. "Really, it will," she continued, coming to stand next to me. "We'll figure it out, okay?" She laid her hand on my arm with a squeeze and pulled the door open. "C'mon." I followed her out into the blinding white day and hoped that she was right.

"Did Sean already go down?" I asked. James jumped, startled by the sound of my voice.

"What? Oh, I don't know. Probably." He turned back to stare down the hill. I sighed in annoyance and glanced at Piper. She shrugged and pointed to the empty sled.

"Have you taken a run yet?" I asked. He shook his head.

"Nah, you go ahead," he mumbled, keeping his eyes off of me.

"It's no fun doing it alone," I whined. "Come with me." I grabbed the sled and held it out, ready for him to hop on. He glanced at it briefly and then back up at me.

"No, thanks," he said shortly. "Piper, you go."

I sucked in my breath and bit my tongue. "Well," I said, my voice cold, "your loss." We sat on the sled and pushed off. The wind whipped my face as I flew down the hill. As we reached the last ridge of the hill, both Piper and I tumbled out of the sled. I lay back in the snow, gazing up at the sky and letting the cold, clean air fill my lungs. Even though it was cold, the sun on my face was pleasant and I closed my eyes, basking in the warmth, rejuvenated by the influx of vitamin D. I propped myself up on my elbows and I looked back up the hill toward the house. A ridge blocked James from view and I could barely see the roof of the cabin.

"You coming?" Piper yelled at me, dragging the sled behind her.

As I walked back up, James and Piper passed me on a sled, laughing and waving. *At least he's lightening up*, I thought as I came over the last ridge. Sean stood there alone.

"Hey," he called, "Where've you been?"

I laughed aloud. "I got lost," I joked. Sean's smile just grew. He gestured toward the remaining empty sled.

"C'mon, take a run with me."

"Sure," I smiled back at him. From there on out, we had a blast. I went down with Piper, Sean, and I even somehow managed to get James to go with me a couple of times. By dinnertime, I thought maybe, just maybe, things could get back to normal between the two of us.

As the sun began to set, the cold deepened and we headed back inside, frozen and starving. Sean ordered a pizza and then he and Piper headed for the hot tub while James and I changed into warm, dry, clothes. I pulled on my hoodie and stood, looking in the bathroom mirror. *I should have brought some make up with me*, I cursed silently. Despite the sunscreen, the sun had turned my face several shades darker pink. I ran my finger along my cheekbone. It wouldn't peel, I decided, but I was going to be pretty uncomfortable for the next twenty-four hours. I sighed and pulled my tangled hair into a ponytail and called it good. I walked out into the living room where James was sitting on the couch.

"Whatcha doing?" I asked, in my best Phineas and Ferb impersonation.

"Reading," James replied shortly. Maybe I should have taken the hint, but I didn't. I wanted to push past this.

"What are you reading?" I asked, settling down on the couch next to him.

He snapped the book shut. "Nothing," he barked, pushing himself off the couch. I glared at him, my hackles rising.

"Okay, I need you to knock it off."

"I don't know what you're talking about," he said shortly, turning away from me, his eyes on the ground. I glanced down the hallway, double-checking that Piper and Sean were out of earshot.

"I'm done, kay? Seriously. It happened and it shouldn't have happened and we both acknowledge that and we're friends again, okay?"

"No," James said shaking his head.

"Why not?" I asked in frustration. "I need you to be my friend. I need you to stop being a jerk."

"This is your fault," he shot at me.

"My fault?" I shot back. "You didn't have to kiss me." I bit my tongue. It was silly to argue this again. "But it doesn't matter. It doesn't matter. I want my friend back."

"No," he said sharply. "No, Sydney," he repeated, standing up and throwing his book down on the coffee table.

"No what?" I snapped, indignant. He glared at me and my heart began to pound.

"No. It's weird. It's different. It's changed." His voice was harsh.

"So what do you want me to do, James? Ignore you? Pretend like I don't know you? Can't we just try this, try to forget what happened, to go back to normal?" I put extra emphasis on the last word. He took a deep breath.

"Do you know that it actually hurts to be in the same room with you?" he said in a low voice. I sucked in my breath sharply, but he kept going. "It's hurt for a long time, but now," he paused, searching for the right words, "it's too much, Sydney." I bit my lip to keep it from quivering. "So, yes. I want you to ignore me. I want you to stop talking to me, to stop texting me, to stop messaging me. I don't really want to see you. Ever."

"James—" I protested, but he cut me off.

"There is no getting back to normal. You're right, it's my fault. I screwed it up. But we're done, Syd. We live in different states. It shouldn't be too hard to avoid each other." His eyes bored into me. A muscle twitched along his jaw. I froze, silently blinking back tears. I felt as if I had been punched in the stomach and then punched again. I wanted to swing back, hurt him like he had hurt me. Once I knew I could keep my voice steady, I spoke.

"If that's what you want, James." I said slowly. "I won't inconvenience you anymore. I'm so sorry to have been such a burden." I hoped that the pain in my voice was audible enough to wound him. "I'll be upstairs until it's time to go." I paused, "That is if you can handle driving home in the same car as me."

He turned to face the windows while I escaped. I held my head high all the way up the stairs, found the nearest bedroom and collapsed on the bed, bawling like a baby. I pulled the covers up over my head to muffle the noise and cried myself to sleep.

When Piper woke me up, the sky was going quickly from pink to gray.

"Syd, what happened? James said you'd be up here." She looked me over as I sat up. "He looks terrible, but you look even worse."

I glared at her. "Gee, thanks." I muttered, rubbing sleep from my eyes.

"No, seriously, what is going on?" she asked again.

I sucked in my breath willing myself not to cry again. "We're done." I answered in a hollow voice.

"Done?"

"James and I. Done." I choked back a sob and covered it, clearing my throat.

"What does that even mean?"

I shook my head. "I screwed up. I thought it was funny, you know? That he had a crush on me. I didn't know . . ." I trailed off.

"I'm sorry, Syd," Piper pulled me into a hug. "You okay?"

I looked at her blankly. "I'm my father's daughter."

"Oh, Sydney." Piper tightened her grip on me. "We need to get going soon. Where's your stuff? I'll pack it up for you."

I smiled my gratitude. "Downstairs bathroom. Hey, Piper," I called her back from the hallway. "Could you and I ride home in the backseat together?"

She smiled. "Sure, anything you want," she called as she disappeared down the stairs.

chapter thirty

NOVEMBER 2017

I stumbled in the front door around 9:00 that night. It had possibly been the longest car ride in the history of my life. I dropped my bag full of snow clothes on the kitchen floor and kicked off my boots. Mom was sitting on the living room floor in her pajamas, reading the newspaper, when I collapsed onto the couch. She studied me for a few minutes.

"Have fun?" she asked, keeping her eyes on me.

"Not really," I said, shifting my gaze to the ceiling.

"What happened?"

I sighed. Where to start? "When you were, you know, still with Dad, before everything, were you happy?"

"What?" she asked, cocking her head to one side. Her long hair fell over one shoulder and she pushed it back.

"Were you happy together? Was he mean? Did you not get along?"

She studied me. "Where is this coming from?"

"Just, were you?"

She looked down at the newspaper for a few moments before responding. "For a while. For a while we were happy. And then, we weren't unhappy, we were just there." She sighed, her eyes still on the floor. "He worked so much and traveled so much. It got to be easier when he wasn't around. Life was smoother when he wasn't here. And he worked with Joanna, and she spent more time with him that I did. I think, in a way, it was bound to happen." She looked up at me. "We didn't really fight. We just kind of stopped speaking to each other. I don't mean the silent treatment; we just stopped talking. Stopped telling each other the little things and the big things. Because I think it got to a point that we didn't care to hear them." She took a deep breath. "What's going on, Sydney?"

"I cheated on Gavin," I said softly, my voice breaking slightly. "I'm no better than Dad."

"Sydney," Mom said. She came and sat next to me on the couch. "What happened? James?"

"How did you know? Did Whitney tell you?" I demanded, ready to disown her for the betrayal.

Mom laughed gently. "Syd, honey, I may be your mom, but I'm not an idiot. James has had a thing for you for a long time. You can see it in his eyes when he looks at you. And while Gavin's on the other side of the country . . ." she trailed off and shrugged.

"I didn't think I was like that, but James kissed me," I took a deep breath, trying to keep my voice even, "and I don't know, Mom."

"Tell me," she encouraged.

"I kissed him back. I wanted him to kiss me again," I admitted reluctantly.

"So, which path are you going to take?" she asked gently.

"I don't know!" I wailed. "I've been with Gavin for three years! He was so great to me," I stopped, "IS so great to me." Mom simply nodded, watching me closely. I readjusted on the couch, nestling closer to her.

"Of course you feel that loyalty to Gavin, and you should. But you are not married. This is not the same."

"It feels the same, Mom," I whispered. She wrapped her arms around me.

"Sydney, you are not a bad person. Just because your father made a terrible mistake does not mean that you are doomed to repeat it." She kissed the crown of my head. "But you are going to have to make a choice. And it won't be an easy one."

"James made it for me. He says it's too hard to be my friend." I swung my legs off the couch and stood. I couldn't talk about it any more. "I'm going to bed," I announced.

She paused and studied my face for a moment. "Syd," she said slowly. "If that is the case, if Gavin is the direction that you choose, he has a right to know." I grimaced.

"What if he doesn't forgive me?" I whispered miserably.

She pursed her lips, thinking. "He might not. He deserves the truth. But, get ready for it. It's going to hurt."

I laughed humorlessly. "Life is pain, Mom. Anyone who says differently is selling something."

She turned offered me a little smile. "Goodnight, sweetie."

"Night," I replied, soberly.

XXX

I arrived back in Boise after Thanksgiving, feeling alone and melancholy. The days seemed to drag by, gray and miserable. I pulled my phone out several times a day to text James—an inside joke, a high grade on a paper—only to slip it back into my pocket with a sick feeling in the pit of my stomach. It was almost as if he had died.

Gavin still texted regularly and I tried, so hard, for the first few weeks to throw myself back into that relationship. We spent more time on the phone than we had all semester, but I found myself with little to say, and it became more and more apparent with each conversation that he was not the one I wanted to talk to.

One night after hanging up with Gavin, I lay on my bed in my apartment, wishing that James had never kissed me, that things could go back to the way that they had been before. As I lay there moping, my roommate Kelsey came in and flopped on her bed.

"You talked to Gavin?" she asked, although it was more of a statement than a question.

"How do you always know?" I asked, turning to look at her. She shrugged.

"You always have that same look on your face." She dumped out her laundry basket on her bed and started folding.

"What look?" I asked, sincerely curious.

"The one that says: I feel awful because I just spent an hour on the phone with my boyfriend and I hated every second of it."

"Ha, ha," I scoffed, rolling my eyes back to the ceiling.

"Why don't you just break it off with him? There are plenty of hot guys to date at BSU. It's not like you only have two options."

I could hear the frustration in her voice. Kelsey and I shared a room and she knew everything. I had come back from Thanksgiving break and spilled. At first, she was incredibly supportive, but after a while, I could tell that I was just dragging her down with me.

"I know," I sighed. "I just feel like I owe him more than that. He was, is so good to me."

"But, why?" she dropped the shirt she was folding and climbed onto my bed with me. "Seriously, Syd. Why? He lives on the other side of the country. You had to know that this relationship was never going to last."

"But—" I began, pulling myself up into a sitting position.

"No," Kelsey cut me off. "But nothing. It's one thing when you can see each other every night. Or even once a week! But this is not high school! You are eighteen years old, a freshman in college, and you haven't gone on one single date! That is just wrong!"

I smiled at her vehemence. "So what do I do?" I asked, "What do I tell him? Do I tell him about James?"

She shook her head. "You're not even speaking to James, so what's the point of that? You just tell him that you feel guilty holding him back. That he should be able to experience college without a girlfriend keeping him tethered down. And if he argues, if he says that he doesn't mind, you tell him that you would rather end it now while you can still be friends, than to end it after he resents you." She paused and looked at me expectantly.

"And if he asks me if there is someone else?" I wondered aloud.

"Look at your life, Syd," she said simply. "There is no one else."

"I'll think about it," I promised. It was all I could do.

And I did, nonstop for the next week. If I did, if I broke up with Gavin, I could really move on. Kelsey was right. There was no one else. James had made that perfectly clear. Staying with Gavin when it was becoming clear that he wasn't the one I wanted to be with wasn't fair to either of us. Maybe Kelsey was right.

✖✖✖

A week or so later, on my way to class, I got a surprise. Sean called. Sean and I were good friends, but phone calls between the two of us were rare, so I was surprised to see his name pop up.

"Hey, what's going on?" I answered.

"Not too much. How are you doing? Finals treating you okay?"

"I don't think it's the finals that are going to kill me, it's the projects," I joked.

"No kidding," he laughed. "That and the papers. I've got a ten page paper due tomorrow, and it will be a miracle if I can get it done."

"Tell me about it," I responded, wondering if he really had just called to chat.

"So, um, I wanted to ask you about something," he began awkwardly. "I was wondering if maybe you could help me figure out what to get Piper for Christmas?"

I laughed. "Sure," I replied. Piper could be difficult to shop for. "What are you thinking?"

"Well," he began slowly. "I saw this necklace that just looks like something she'd like, but I wondered if you could look at it and tell me what you think. I can send you the link. If you have time," he added hesitantly. "But I don't know. Is jewelry too much?"

I laughed again. "For Piper? Never."

He sighed with relief. "Good. Thanks. And, um, hey, do you think we could not mention this to Piper?"

"You have my word." I paused, silently debating about asking what I wanted to know. "Hey, Sean, can I ask you something?"

"Sure," he said, surprised.

"Did you know? About . . . That James . . ." I trailed off, trying to decide how to say it.

"That he had a thing for you?" Sean finished. "Yeah. I did."

"How long?" I asked softly. There was a pause. I had reached the art building where my class was, but stopped outside, not wanting to cut the conversation short.

"A while," Sean responded, vaguely. "Why?"

"Did Gavin know?"

"No," Sean responded quickly. "No, Gavin never knew." He paused. "We both figured out that it would be best not to tell Gavin."

"Why didn't James ever tell me?" I asked.

"Sydney, he didn't . . . he thought, well, he thought it was too late."

"Sean?" I asked again, hesitating. "Have you talked to him?"

"Gavin?" he asked, hopefully.

"James."

I could hear him sigh in exasperation over the phone. "Yeah," he replied.

"And?"

"He's fine," he said.

"Oh," I replied, feigning nonchalance. "Okay. Good."

"He works like a maniac and when he's not working or in class, he's running." Sean let out a mirthless laugh. "In short, he's miserable." It was quiet for a minute. I don't know what I expected. I should never have asked. It didn't make anything any easier.

"I have class, Sean, I have to go." I blurted, unable to stay on the phone a minute longer.

"Right," he said, "I'll text you that link then."

"Sounds great," I replied.

"Thanks again, Syd." he said. "See you at Christmas?"

"Sure. Bye." I hit end and trudged up the stairs of the art building, trying not to think how stupid it was for both of us to be so miserable.

December was long and cold and arduous. Freshman finals were more than I was expecting, and I barely kept my head above water. I had to put together a portfolio for my final project in Intro to Graphic Design. It took hours and hours in the computer lab, working on a faster, more powerful computer than my laptop. Finally, I put the finishing touches on it, mere hours before it was due. I was just finishing up when the screen suddenly went black. I yelped and wiggled the mouse, hoping that the screensaver was just freaking out. No luck. I checked the power button but the light was off. My heart dropped. I flipped the switch to turn it back on and waited for the computer to restart. It was the longest three minutes of my life. I clicked on the design program and opened it back up, but the file was gone.

"No," I whispered, staring at the screen in horror. "No, no, no, no, no, no!" My voice got louder with each "no," until those surrounding me began to stare; some with sympathy, others in annoyance. I clapped my hand over my mouth to keep myself from distracting anyone else and clicked frantically on the screen, trying desperately to get back everything that had just been erased. I swallowed the panic and tried everything that I could think of to retrieve the file. I glanced around the room, searching for a familiar face, someone in my program that might have some secret trick that would solve my problem. No one. I stared at the screen, thinking about how long it had taken me to complete that assignment, and the thought of starting from scratch was painful, and honestly, impossible. As a last desperate attempt, I grabbed my phone and hit Gavin's number. Leaving my bag next to my computer, I went out into the hall, waiting for Gavin to pick up.

"Hello?" I heard, after what seemed like a hundred rings.

"Gavin," I begged, "What do you know about Illustrator?"

"What, Syd? Illustrator? I don't know. That's your thing. Why?" His voice was impatient. I had no idea what time it was in Connecticut.

"I just lost my entire portfolio," I choked, desperately fighting off the anxiety attack.

"Hey, Syd, that really sucks. But I'm in the middle of something and I need to go. Can I call you later?"

"Um, sure," I said, fighting back tears of disappointment. Really though, I told myself, he's on the other side of the country. What could he really have done?

"Great. Bye." I looked at my phone in disbelief. Below Gavin's name in my Favorites was James. I hit it in desperation and he answered on the second ring.

"Sydney?" he answered.

"I need help," I gushed, panic soaking my words.

"Where are you? What's wrong?" he asked immediately, his tone concerned.

"I accidentally lost my entire portfolio," I gasped, really struggling to keep sobs of panic down.

"Sydney, calm down. It's gonna be okay." James's voice was even and calm. Just the sound of it made my anxiety level drop a little.

"No," I responded, distraught. "It's not. It's due tonight and it's half of my grade."

"What were you working in?" he asked.

"Illustrator. The computer shut down by itself and it just disappeared. I'm so screwed," I whimpered.

"Syd, stop," he said reassuring me. "My friend's a computer genius. I'm on campus right now. I'll stop by and call you back. Relax. It'll be okay."

"Thank you, James." I said softly.

"You're welcome." His voice was suddenly clipped. "I'll talk to you in a minute." He hung up. I stood in the empty hallway trying to get my breathing under control. I headed back to the lab, but before I could get there, my phone rang.

"James?" I answered.

"Listen, Syd. Does Illustrator automatically save changes?"

I thought for a moment. "Um, no, I don't think so," I stammered.

"Good," he replied. From there he talked me through the process of retrieving my project, echoing the instructions conveyed by his friend. Five minutes later I was ready to cry again, this time tears of relief.

"James," I said, trying to avoid the wrath of fellow computer lab patrons. "Thank you. I owe you one." The line was momentarily silent.

"No, you don't."

"James," I began hesitantly, "I'm so sorry. I didn't know who else to call—" he cut me off.

"Don't, Sydney. Just. . . . I'm glad I could help."

"Right. Well, um, thanks again." We hung up and I saved my portfolio in three different places before heading out to turn it in. I walked home slowly, feeling worse than I had since the night at the cabin.

XXX

As the month wore on, my communication with Gavin became more and more perfunctory, and I blamed it on finals, though, to be honest, my heart wasn't really in it any more. I finally decided that after Christmas, before Gavin had to go back to school, I would end it. I had a speech all ready for him. This long distance relationship isn't working, I need to focus on school right now, I don't want to hold you back, I hope we can still be friends. And while all those reasons were good, that wasn't why I was doing it. I was terrified, but determined: I didn't want to waste any more of his time, or mine.

I told Piper my plan a few days before the semester ended. I hit a wall and couldn't study for one more second, so I pulled out my phone and called her, hoping to catch her between finals as well. The gods, it seemed, were on our side because she answered on the third ring. She was surprised to hear from me; we usually communicated by email or text. But I didn't think I could explain this with emojis.

"I'm going to wait until after Christmas to do it," I explained, "that way, I don't totally ruin the holiday for him."

"Do you have to break up with him?" she whined. "You're totally going to ruin our New Year's Eve plans."

Ever grateful for her supportive attitude, I snorted. "You're going to be with Sean. You're hardly even going to notice who's there," I pointed out drily. "And honestly, the entire holiday is going to suck, because you know that James is going to avoid coming anywhere that I might be."

She sighed. "It's true. Well, at least you're going to wait until after Christmas. Why don't you just wait until he goes back and email him?"

"Because I'm more mature than you are."

"And more boring," she shot back.

"Shut up."

"When do you get home?" she asked lightly.

"Friday night. What about you?"

"My flight comes in on Monday morning. Both my parents will be at work. I can't decide. Do you want to come pick me up, or should I have Sean do it?"

"Are you really asking me this?"

"Well, I don't want to smell like airplane when I see him for the first time in a month."

I snorted again. This was a fantastic study break. "What?" she asked, genuinely confused. "I'll go home and shower and then I can see him."

"I would love to pick you up on Monday morning. What time?"

"10:15."

"Okay. I'm glad you're crazy." I joked.

"Whatever. Love you."

"Love you too. See you soon."

chapter thirty-one

DECEMBER 2017

My phone lit up with a text. I reached down into my purse to pull it out.

"Is that my phone?" Kelsey asked, keeping her eyes on the road. She was heading home to Vegas, and had been gracious enough to agree to take me home on her way.

"Mine." I opened the text. "Gavin wants me to come pick him up from the airport tomorrow." I sighed and dropped the phone back into my purse. She glanced at me briefly.

"So, did you decide what to do?"

"I think I'm going to take your advice." I said slowly.

"Sooner than later, right?" she asked.

I nodded. "I'm going to wait until after Christmas, I think. But, yeah."

"It really is for the best, you know."

"I know," I replied. "Doesn't make it any easier."

"Nope." She smiled. "Just focus on winter semester. Let that be your happy place."

"What?" I asked laughing. "I mean, I like school and all, but I don't really think it qualifies as my happy place."

"Not school so much, as all the dating that you're going to do once you get back here."

I laughed aloud. "Because boys will be falling all over themselves to date me?"

"No," she grinned, "because I'm going to set you up with pretty much everyone I know."

"Definitely something to look forward to." I paused at the thought of many, many awkward blind dates. "I think."

The next morning I woke up sweating. I glanced at my alarm clock on the nightstand. 4:52. I rolled back over, exhausted but unable to go back to sleep. The idea of seeing Gavin in person was nerve-racking. The internal debate of whether or not to tell Gavin about what happened between James and me, and the anticipation of the breakup, was even worse. Part of me wanted to tell him, just tell the truth and get it over with. The other part of me was terrified. Just simply terrified. The thought of hurting Gavin like that was horrible. That, and the fact that Gavin had never lost his temper with me, and I wasn't looking forward to having that happen.

I tried in vain for another hour to go back to sleep before I padded down to the living room and flipped on the TV. I settled on an old infomercial for the Magic Bullet and stared blankly at the TV, trying to forget about the day I had ahead of me. The Magic Bullet failed to hold my attention, and somewhere between smoothies and baby food I dozed off.

I woke with a jolt at the sound of dishes clanking in the kitchen. I sat up quickly. Mom was in the kitchen, unloading the dishwasher.

"What time is it?" I asked, panicked. She glanced behind her at the clock on the microwave.

"9:15," she replied.

"Crap!" I blurted as I jumped off the couch. "I'm supposed to be at the airport in twenty minutes!" I ran down the hallway to my room, realizing that there was no time for a shower. I pulled on some clean clothes, covered myself in Victoria Secret body spray, and prayed that would be enough, at least for this morning. After a quick swipe of mascara, I grabbed a hat to cover the worst of my bed head and I was out the door.

The airport was packed. Gavin obviously wasn't the only one coming home for the holidays. It had taken ten minutes to find a parking space, and Gavin had texted me, telling me that his plane had landed, and which baggage claim to meet him at. I booked it through the parking garage and down the crowded moving sidewalk. My eyes were on the baggage claim numbers, rather than the crowd, as I walked through the terminal. *There it is*, I thought with relief. Baggage claim number seven. Now that I knew where I was going, my eyes began to scan the crowd, looking for a sign of Gavin. They didn't find him. They did, however, land on James. He stood next to the carousel, hands in his jacket pockets. His dark hair was a mess, he had obviously just rolled out of bed as well, and his eyes were on me. I stopped abruptly, staring at him. I sucked in my breath, realizing suddenly just how much I had missed him, how much it hurt to see him standing there. I took a deep breath and began walking again. I kept my eyes on the ground as I approached, wondering what was going on inside of his head.

"Hi," I murmured as I reached him.

"Hey," he replied gently. I wanted so badly to talk to him, to tell him how much I had missed him, to hug him. But we both stood silently, keeping our eyes on each other, trying to find words.

"Sydney—" he began, but was cut off.

"You guys!" came a familiar voice. "Over here!" I ripped my eyes away from James to where Gavin was waving, and plastered a smile on my face.

"Gavin!" I cried, hurrying over. I threw my arms around him and put on a great show of welcoming him home. He pressed his lips against mine and I was so very aware of James standing next to us. I pulled away. "Look, James is here!" I announced, unnecessarily. James's forced smile mirrored mine as he slugged Gavin on the shoulder.

"Hey, man," he said. "Welcome home."

Gavin looked around us curiously. "No Sean or Piper?" he asked.

"Piper doesn't get home until Monday," I replied.

"Sean had to work," James added.

"Your parents didn't come?" I asked, glancing around looking for them. Gavin shook his head.

"I'll see enough of them over the holiday. I wanted to see you guys," he added, putting his arm around my waist and pulling me close. I squeezed him awkwardly and pulled away as the luggage began to spin around the carousel.

"Hey, isn't that yours?" I asked, walking to the carousel and pointing to a large black suitcase.

"No, not that one," Gavin replied, walking to stand next to me. "It's that one . . ." he pointed, trailing off. The suitcase that had just come off of the conveyor belt was ripped across the front, the contents spilling out. "Are you kidding me?" Gavin spat. He yanked it off of the claim. I grabbed a pair of pants off of the belt that had fallen out of the destroyed suitcase. Gavin sat rifling through it, checking for missing items. "I can't believe this!" he exclaimed angrily.

"Take it to the baggage claims office," advised James, pointing to a door just down from the carousel. "They should at least be able to reimburse you for it." Gavin glanced up and nodded, gathering the destroyed suitcase in his arms. James picked up a couple of books and I grabbed a shirt and we all headed in that direction. The office was tiny. Once Gavin was in there with his suitcase, there was no room for me or James.

"We'll just wait right out here. Good luck!" I encouraged. Gavin offered an ironic smile and went to yell at someone else. James and I stood awkwardly just outside the doorway. After a few moments of silence, we both began talking at once.

"I'm sorry, I didn't know—"

"I should have checked—"

We both stopped and looked at each other. I smiled slightly. "I didn't know you were going to be here," I said. "But," I paused, debating, "it's good to see you."

"It's good to see you too," he replied hoarsely. Our eyes locked and it seemed like there was so much to say but words were so inadequate.

"I've missed you," I breathed. A spasm of pain blew across his face. "I'm sorry," I whispered, taking a step back. "I shouldn't have . . ." I backed into Gavin coming out of the office, his suitcase now wrapped in heavy-duty plastic wrap. I swallowed hard.

Gavin held up the remains of his suitcase. "This was the best they could do for me, but they'll supposedly replace it," he announced, obviously annoyed.

"Let's get out of here," I replied. "It won't be so depressing once you get home."

"Sydney," said James formally, "will you take Gavin home? I need to get to work."

"Sure," I replied, my voice still annoyingly cheerful. "I would love to."

Gavin raised his eyebrows at us. "You guys didn't come together?" he asked.

We both glanced at each other. "I overslept," I replied quickly. "So I told James to come without me because I didn't want you to have to wait."

James nodded sycophantically. "Yeah, plus I have to work in a bit, so Syd can take you home."

"Right," I agreed, grateful for the excuse.

"Okay," Gavin accepted our story without question. "We'll hang out tonight then."

"Sure," James responded. "See you tonight."

Gavin and I walked to the car together, his arms wrapped around his suitcase. I popped the trunk and he threw it in angrily. I put my hand lightly on his arm and he surprised me by throwing his arms around me and pulling me close. He tucked his head into my neck and breathed deeply.

"I have been waiting forever to do that," he said huskily. I squeezed back and ran my fingers through his short hair. "I missed you," he continued. He pulled back to kiss me full on the mouth. It made me wonder momentarily if I had made the right decision or not.

XXX

As we drove to James's that night, Gavin was quiet. "You know," he observed after a long while, "I've noticed something since I've been gone. When I tell you I love you, you never say it back."

"Yes I do!" I exclaimed, affronted. "Every time."

Gavin shook his head. "No," he said slowly. "You never say 'I love you.' Always just 'you too.' And you never say it first." He paused. "I was reading your texts the other night. That's when I realized it."

"No, I'm sure I do," I protested, thinking hard. "Don't I?"

"Why do you do that?" he asked slowly. The sight of James and Sean standing on James's porch saved me from trying to answer. As we pulled into the driveway, Sean galloped down the steps to greet Gavin. James remained on the porch, watching us. I followed Sean and Gavin into the house; James was close behind.

We sat around James's living room, debating how to spend the rest of the evening. I had already attempted to excuse myself, giving the boys a chance to spend the night playing Halo without distraction, but Gavin was adamant that I stick around. Gavin was throwing out suggestions while the rest of us sat awkwardly, glancing at each other sporadically. Gavin seemed to be completely oblivious to the uncomfortable atmosphere as he listed the possibilities.

"We could get dinner? Go see Christmas lights? How about a movie?"

The rest of us halfheartedly agreed to a movie. James's laptop was sitting on the end table next to Gavin. "Mind if I look up times?" Gavin asked James, pulling it into his lap. "I'm totally out of data on my phone."

"Sure," James agreed. Gavin flipped it opened and waited until it lit up.

"Where's your—" Gavin began, "Never mind, I found it." He clicked around for a minute. "Okay. This looks good. 8:00," he glanced up at the clock on the wall. "We can make that. Sound okay to you guys?" We all mumbled our consent.

Gavin clicked the browser closed and paused, staring at the screen. "Syd?" he asked slowly, "Did you borrow James's computer?"

"What?" I perked up, "No, why?" I leaned over to try and catch a glimpse of the screen.

"There's a file on here with your name on it." I looked over at James, my eyes wide and questioning. His expression betrayed his panic and he quickly stood.

"Hey, if we're going to catch that movie, we should get going. It's almost eight," he said loudly, reaching for the laptop. Gavin shifted it quickly out of reach.

"Oh, yeah, we need to go," I agreed in the same tone, hopping off of the couch, attempting to close the computer in the process. It didn't quite work. Gavin's eyes narrowed as he clicked through the file.

"James? What is this?" he asked, his voice hard. James reached out again for the laptop, but Gavin pulled it out of his reach. "'Forget everything I said at the cabin. I want to see you again, kiss you again.' What the heck, James?"

I gasped, feeling as if I had been punched in the gut. "It's nothing . . . nothing," James stuttered, reaching unsuccessfully for the computer.

"That isn't nothing," Gavin continued reading. "'You mean everything to me, Sydney.'" Gavin glanced at me. My shocked expression didn't do much to help the situation. "What is going on?" His voice rose as he spoke. "Did you even wait until I got on the plane?"

James threw up his hands, almost as if in surrender. "It isn't like that, Gavin. It was never like that. There's nothing going on."

Gavin snorted in disbelief. "Your letter says differently."

"Gavin," I began hoarsely, "it was one time. Just one time. It was so late," I stammered, barely able to catch my breath, "and it was Thanksgiving—"

Gavin cut me off with an ironic laugh. "Right. Oh, and look, pictures. How sweet." His voice was acid.

"What?" I screeched, my eyes flying back to James. "Pictures?"

He stood abruptly and dumped the laptop onto the couch.

"Listen, Gavin, she's telling the truth—" James trailed off at the look on Gavin's face.

"Go to heck," Gavin said. He brushed past me and I jumped as the front door slammed shut. I glanced at James briefly before turning to follow Gavin out of the house. He was already in the car, rolling down the driveway. I ran to the driver's side, pounding on the window.

"Gavin!" I yelled, "Please. Please! Just let me explain!" The car didn't stop and after one long hard glare, Gavin didn't look at me again. "I'm sorry!" I yelled desperately, "I'm so sorry!" my voice crackling with emotion. I watched the car until I couldn't see it anymore. I stood at the end of the driveway in the cold, my mind racing.

"Sydney?" a voice said quietly behind me. James laid his hand lightly on my arm. I wrenched it out of his grip.

"Don't." Both of us were surprised by the ice in my voice. James crossed his arms in front of his chest and took a step back. His breath escaped in little clouds in the cold air.

"Syd," he said again.

"No," I looked him in the face. "What pictures, James?" I spat.

"Pictures?"

"Don't be stupid. On your computer. What pictures?" My eyes bored into him. He turned his gaze to his feet.

"You've seen them. Most of them. From Lake Blanche. From the Salt Flats. They're all of you. Of us."

"He was reading a letter. What was it?" My voice was still harsh. I noticed for the first time my fingernails digging into the palms of my hands. James kept his eyes down and his voice dropped. He took another step away from me.

"It was for you." I could barely hear him as he spoke. "To apologize." A letter. About us. I wasn't sure if I was flattered or curious or disgusted. All of a sudden I was exhausted. "Sydney—" he tried again, but I cut him off.

"I'm tired, James, will you please take me home?" He nodded soberly and returned to the house to get his keys. I stood alone in the driveway, waiting for him and staring down the street. Despite everything, I realized I was almost relieved that it was over with Gavin. I felt sick that it had happened like it did, and that we had hurt Gavin so horribly. I wished he would just listen to an explanation. I glanced down at my hands and realized they were shaking. James reappeared in a jacket with keys in hand. We drove to my house in silence. He pulled his car into the driveway and turned to look at me.

"I'm really sorry, Sydney. I didn't mean . . ." he trailed off and turned to gaze out the windshield. "I feel like I've ruined everything for you," he said.

I laughed wryly. "Well," I said, agreeing with him.

"I could go talk to him, Syd. I could tell him it was all me, that you did nothing wrong—"

I cut him off. "You know that he will never listen to you. He'll shut the door in your face and never speak to you again."

"Sean knows," James tried desperately. "If Sean could talk to him, maybe convince him to take you back . . ." he trailed off.

I hesitated a moment before speaking. "I was going to break up with him," I said, keeping my gaze out past the windshield. "After Christmas. I had a whole speech planned out. How I was holding him back. How it was so hard to manage a long distance relationship." I sighed. "It was a good speech too." I reached for the door handle.

"Sydney—" For the first time his voice wavered.

"I've gotta go. I'll see—" I began, but realized that I didn't know if I would see him again. I took a deep breath. "Bye, James." I amended, pulling myself out of the car.

"Bye, Sydney." I could hear the sadness in his voice, but I was still so upset that I didn't care. I shut the door and walked into the house without looking back.

chapter thirty-two

JANUARY 1, 2017

James and I let ourselves into my dark house just after midnight. Whitney was at a party and Tyler and Mom had obviously gone to bed at the stroke of midnight. The majority of the evening had been spent party hopping, but as the final hour of the year drew near, Piper and Sean decided they wanted to spend the midnight hour alone, and since Gavin was spending the holiday in Hawaii with his family, James came home with me after the ball dropped. Both of us had extended curfews for one night only, and neither of us were ready for the night to be over. I pulled out the sparkling cider Mom had gotten for Tyler and a huge bag of chips.

James sat on the couch and I collapsed next to him, draping my legs over his and handing him the bag of chips to open. I grabbed the two glasses of cider off the coffee table and handed him one.

"Happy new year," he said quietly, holding his glass out to me. I clinked mine against his and smiled.

"Happy new year." I took a long drink and studied him. "So, I tried to be tactful and everything, but I gotta know. Why are you not hanging out with your girlfriend tonight?" I popped another chip in my mouth. James had been together with a girl from school for about a month, but I hadn't seen her at all over Christmas break. I had managed to bite my tongue until tonight, but my decorum had been dampened by exhaustion.

He shrugged slightly. "We broke it off the other day." He was very nonchalant about the whole thing. I pushed myself up on my elbows.

"What? What happened?" I asked curiously. He wrinkled his nose at me.

"She was a little too drama for me," he replied, taking a sip of cider.

"So you ended it?" I pursued.

"It was her," he said slowly. "But it's no big deal." He raised his eyebrows at me. "Why? You got somebody in mind to set me up with?"

"Ha, ha," I laughed dryly, handing him the bag of chips and nestling myself further into the couch.

James lifted his head off of the back of the couch, looked at me and smiled. "You should go to bed," he advised, patting my knee gently. "You look exhausted."

I could barely lift my head, but I wasn't about to admit that. "No," I replied, stifling a yawn. "I'm not tired at all. I could run a race right now," I joked. His smile grew.

"Really? Well, let's go!" He pretended to push my legs off of him.

"Ugh, I forgot you're a runner freak," I teased. "Let's watch a movie, instead. You want to watch a movie?" I asked. This time he laughed out loud.

"Sure, what?"

I was struggling to keep my eyes open. The Princess Bride. *I murmured.*

"Again?" he moaned.

"It's my favorite." I gave him my best puppy dog smile. "'Far off places, daring swordfights, magic spells. A prince in disguise.'" He shook his head at me.

"You're impossible."

"I know." I grabbed the remote and switched on the TV. Peter Falk's voice filled the room. James pulled a blanket over the two of us. Things began to get really fuzzy. I managed to watch the beginning, and be disappointed all over again when Westley's ship is attacked, but after that, things went pretty dark. I fell asleep on the couch and began to dream. I dreamt that James stood up, tucked the blanket around me and kissed my forehead as he left. And then he was in a sword fight and I was in the fire swamp. And things didn't really make sense after that. When I woke up the next morning, I was alone on the couch, wondering how much of that had been real.

chapter thirty-three

DECEMBER 2017

My Christmas break was not particularly filled with joy. I vacillated constantly between missing James, feeling guilty about Gavin, and trying to work up the courage to discuss future college prospects with my mom. I had avoided the subject since I had been home, trying to delay the bad news as long as possible. Six months ago, I had been willing to stay home, help out, and go to school here. Today, I wanted nothing more than to be back in Idaho. I did get a lot of reading done and I drew and designed almost constantly. I wasn't surprised at how often James and Gavin tended to turn up in my work.

The day before Christmas Eve I found my mom watching a movie in her bed. She had today and tomorrow off, but she would have to work Christmas day. We would open presents tomorrow and then Christmas night we'd go to my Aunt Becca's for dinner without her.

"Are you busy?" I asked tentatively from her doorway. She glanced up at me and paused her movie. I glanced at the screen. *"Pride and Prejudice?"*

"Mr. Darcy forever," she laughed. I sat down next to her on the bed.

"Um," I said slowly, hating to put her on the spot. "Have you talked to Dad any more?"

She sighed. "A little bit."

"And?"

"I still don't know, Sydney. And I know," she responded to my expression, "tuition is due in like two weeks. I honestly don't know what to tell you." Her voice cracked just slightly as she spoke and my heart sank. I was quiet, my mind racing over all the possible alternatives I had come up with over the past six weeks.

"Okay," I said resolutely, "okay. My dorm is paid through the year. The school has tuition payment plans. If we can cover one month, I can get a student loan or I can get a second job."

"Sydney," Mom began but I cut her off.

"I'll just figure it out, and it'll be fine."

Mom's face was red at the effort of holding back tears. "I'm so sorry, sweetie," she said, a sob breaking free. "I really wanted to give this to you."

I moved closer to her on the bed and wrapped my arms around her. "It's not your fault," I replied, my own voice shaky. I grabbed the remote and started the movie again. I nestled into the blankets and we watched Elizabeth fall in love with Mr. Darcy for the hundredth time.

XXX

My phone was remarkably quiet through the three weeks I was home, with only occasional texts from Piper or my family. I sent Gavin several long apologies, but unsurprisingly got no response.

The week after Christmas, Whitney was gone most days working at the mall during the day and she spent all of her time with friends at night. I played a little bit of Xbox with Tyler, and one night Piper and Beth came over for a movie night. We watched *Love Actually* and *New Year's Eve* and I went to bed feeling more lonely and depressed than ever.

I spent long hours at the computer, applying to every available job in Boise. I was limited to employment that I could walk to, and something on campus would be a straight up miracle. I also researched student loans and bookmarked the least shady options, hoping never to have to find it again.

The whole week between holidays was tedious, but New Year's Eve might have been the very worst. Piper begged me to come party hopping with her and Sean, but I couldn't stomach the thought of running into Gavin or James, or heaven forbid, both, at one of the many parties that I knew Piper and Sean would be hitting that night.

"You know I'm just going to be a third wheel," I told her. "You only have a few days before you have to head back to school and you're going to want to stay in California over spring break. You might as well make the most of it and I'll just be in your way."

Piper smiled sadly at me. "You're too nice for your own good," she said. She knew I was lying; she knew the real reason I didn't come. She was just too good of a friend to point it out. Instead, she hugged me and made me promise to call around noon the next day.

I stayed home with Tyler watching movies. My mom had to work and Whitney went party hopping with her new boyfriend. Tyler and I made it through *Star Wars* and *The Empire Strikes Back* before Tyler fell asleep on the floor around 11:00. I lay on the couch, curled up in a blanket and debating about heading to bed myself, despite how pathetic that was, but finally I turned on *The Princess Bride* instead. I watched Wesley and Buttercup and thought about Gavin and James.

My eyes fell on my phone, lying on top of the coffee table. I picked it up and began scrolling through old texts from Gavin. Most were perfunctory, 'I miss you,' 'I'm thinking about you,' or 'what are you doing?' with a few 'I love you's scattered throughout. I switched to James's texts and smiled. There were a few 'how are you?' texts, but most were totally random thoughts. One day he texted me,

You know what's ironic? The *Star Wars* commercials are mostly scenes from the originals. Why? No one cares about the first three.

And another day,

Random person on the side of the road, holding a sign: *Zombies ate my family. Need money for ammunition.*

And finally,

Can you hold my hammer for me? My arm is so Thor.

I smiled reading the last one. It had arrived in the middle of a really rough day right before midterms. He always somehow knew. I stared at my phone willing him to text me.

The front door slammed shut and Whitney appeared. She plopped down next to me on the couch. "Why do you like this movie so much?" she asked staring at the screen.

"I don't know," I muttered. "I just do."

She glanced at me and then back at the screen. "I mean, it's funny and everything. A lot of great lines. But Buttercup is kind of a wimp."

I sat up. "What?" I asked, totally offended.

"Seriously," Whitney said. "Think about it. Westley dies. She basically gives up on life. Evil prince wants to marry her. Sure, what-ever. Westley wants to fight to the death for her, she's like nope, too hard. Then, she just waits around for him to come save her, and when she thinks he's not coming, she plans on killing herself."

I leaned back against the arm of the couch equally irritated at having my favorite movie unpacked so thoroughly and annoyed at myself for never having noticed it. "She jumps out of the boat, to escape. She had to have a little courage for that, right?"

"One moment in an entire movie does not a heroine make," Whitney shot back. She shrugged and stood up. "I don't particularly want to be like Buttercup, but that's just me." She disappeared down the hallway and I heard her bedroom door shut.

Was that me? I thought in consternation. Was I just waiting around to be saved just to give up when it didn't come? I was not a damsel in distress. I would get a job, I would get a loan, I would get a degree. And James? James was only a phone call away. I wanted my friend back. The worst had happened: I had lost them both. There couldn't be more fallout, and all I wanted at this moment was to hear James's voice. I glanced at the clock. 12:30. I had missed the count-down, but I really didn't care. I was done waiting.

I grabbed my phone, James was still in my favorites. Just as I was about to hit send, there was a knock on the front door. I stood up slowly, shedding my blanket. It was probably just Piper, stopping to say hi on her way home. I walked down the hall, flipping on lights as I went. I peered out the peephole and took a step backward in shock. Gavin stood there, waiting, his hands stuffed into his coat pockets. I took a deep breath and pulled the door open slowly.

"Gavin?"

He gave me a sheepish smile. "I know it's late, but I figured tonight it would be okay," he shrugged. "I've missed you, Sydney." He glanced at my face, hopeful.

I opened the door wider, and the cold air that rushed in almost took my breath away, but I didn't invite him in. "What are you doing here?" I asked. He looked disappointed by my lack of excitement.

He pulled one hand out of his pocket and pulled at his ear nervously. "I ran into James tonight," he began. "Well, he cornered me actually. At Will's party. Wanted me to know that he was sorry and that it was all on him. He said you hadn't done anything wrong. He

181

told me that he had kissed you in a moment of stupidity and you both felt so terrible about it that nothing else had ever happened. He promised me that nothing else would ever happen again. I still kind of wanted to punch him, but I've missed you so much that it was good to hear." He paused, studying me. "I had to see you," he added, searching my face. "I want you back."

I stared at him blankly. This was the last thing that I had expected tonight. I swallowed and gripped the doorknob tightly.

"What?" I asked, trying to regain my bearings.

He took a deep breath. "I miss you. I love you. I want you back." He reached out his hand for mine, but I pulled back. Gavin flinched.

"No," I whispered.

Gavin's eyebrows furrowed in confusion. "What?" he asked.

I cleared my throat and spoke again, louder this time. "No, Gavin."

"No, what? No, James was lying or no, you don't want to get back together?"

I heard the anger blossoming in his voice and I bit my lip, bracing myself for the impending storm. "Gavin," I paused, gathering courage. "I should have told you. When it happened. With James. I should have told you then, and I'm so, so sorry that you had to find out the way that you did. I didn't tell you because I couldn't stand the thought of hurting you. And he was telling the truth, nothing else happened. I need you to know that." I gazed at him, emphasizing my apology with my eyes. I hoped he understood as I continued. "But, I don't want to get back together," I said firmly, surprised by the resolve in my voice. "It's not James. We've barely spoken since, but I don't—" I broke off and swallowed hard, struggling to say it again. "I don't want to be together." I looked at him, pleading with my eyes to just leave, to understand, to let me be. I didn't get my wish.

"I don't understand, Sydney," he said harshly. "I love you. I thought you loved me. I figured that you would want me back. That you would have missed me as much as I missed you." His voice grew in volume and anger. "Why are you doing this?"

"I'm sorry, Gavin. I'm so sorry. But I can't. I, I don't." I stammered. "Goodnight." I started to close the door, but he put his hand out to stop it. I didn't force it, I just looked at him sadly.

"I deserve at least to know why. Is it someone else? Is it James? Is that why? At least have the decency to tell me the truth." He was shouting now. I glanced back into the house, hoping that Tyler wouldn't wake up. I looked back at Gavin, trying to form into words the reason that I was saying no to him. I thought momentarily about the speech that I had practiced over and over in my head.

"We're not . . . It's not fair . . ." I began and stopped. He was right, he deserved the truth, as painful as it might be. "I don't . . . I don't love you," I said softly. "I'm so sorry."

Gavin looked as if I had slapped him across the face. It was worse than I thought it would be, worse than him storming away, cursing. He stood speechless for a moment before turning around to walk down the driveway without looking back. I watched him go, watched him get into his car and drive away. I closed the door gently, and glanced down at my phone, still clutched in my hand. I stared at it in defeat, then locked the door, padded silently down the dark hall, and slid into bed.

chapter thirty-four

JANUARY 2018

Kelsey had picked me up on her way back from Vegas after Christmas and during the five-hour car ride back to Boise, I told her everything. Well, almost everything.

I didn't tell her about the two days I spent in bed. I didn't tell her about the text from James that simply read, "I'm sorry." And I didn't tell her about the conversation with my mom that had finally pushed me back on my feet.

"Do you remember," she began, sitting on the edge of my bed, "when you were about twelve and we went water skiing with Aunt Becca and Uncle Steve?" Mom asked. I nodded wondering what that had to do with anything. "You couldn't get up on the skis."

I grimaced. "I remember. It was kind of humiliating. And frustrating."

"You tried for a long time, but you could never quite get it. And then when you were done trying, the boat came to get you and you had a horrible time trying to pull yourself in."

"This is a great pep talk, Mom." I retorted sarcastically. "You really know how to encourage a girl."

Mom smiled. "When you couldn't get in the boat, your cousins tried to help you."

"Yep. Austin and Patrick jumped into the lake to help me out." I snorted. The twelve- and fourteen-year-old boys were doing nothing more than showing off.

"But you didn't let them."

I shook my head. "No. I was already embarrassed enough that I couldn't ski, I wasn't about to let stupid Patrick manhandle me back into the boat."

"You didn't need anyone else to get you back in the boat then, and you don't need anyone now. It was hard to lose James; it was hard to lose Gavin. Don't let it be hard anymore, Sydney. Get back in the boat."

The words echoed through the rest of the weekend and followed me into the car with Kelsey. "So, what are you going to do?" Kelsey asked.

"About what?" I asked.

Kelsey snorted. "Any of it."

Mom and I had scraped enough together for an initial tuition payment. "I've got three job interviews set up for the first week I'm back; if none of them work out I'll take out a loan."

Kelsey glanced over at me. "And then what?"

I shook my head. "I don't know. I was hoping to transfer to Cal Arts next year, but I think I might transfer down to the U. I don't have to pay housing and I can take the train to school. It'll be easier to get a job down there too." I sighed. "Maybe I'll just wait and do my master's at Cal Arts and spend the next four years saving up for it."

"Well," she said slowly, "If you do get a job too far to walk to, your welcome to borrow the car."

"Thanks, Kels," I replied gratefully. "That is so nice of you."

She glanced at me, a sly look on her face. "I will require some form of payment," she said with a smile.

"Like what?" I asked suspiciously.

"Well," she said slowly, "if you're sure you have James out of your system—"

"I do," I interrupted a little too quickly. She glanced at me.

"And you're willing to overlook the intense letter he wrote to you proclaiming his love—"

"That he never sent—"

"And that everything he said up to that point had been fake, then I'm going to require that you start going out. With boys. That I set you up with." She gave me her most charming smile.

I laughed. "Hit me with your best shot," I said.

"Oh, I plan to," she replied, grinning back.

And so, every weekend for the past month, I have been set up on more dates than I can count. All of them blind, a few of them dismal failures that will one day become great party anecdotes, and a few with potential of repeat.

January in Boise is cold. It's not very wet, but the wind is frigid. Walking to class was torture. Walking to work was even worse. After bombing my three interviews, a friend in one of my classes told me that the school was hiring janitorial staff. It would require working from 4:00 a.m. to 7:00 a.m. four days a week, but it didn't interfere with my classes or my schedule at Einstein's. And, if I ate PB and J and tuna fish almost exclusively, I could afford to finish out the semester. I was a walking zombie most of the time, but it was worth it.

XXX

About a week before Valentine's Day, Kelsey came into our room and plopped on my bed while I was studying. I glanced up from my books. History and biology were over, but I was dealing with math this semester and it was killing me.

"Are you here as a distraction or assistance?" I asked as she gazed over the books lying between us.

"Mostly distraction. But I can help if you want me to," she replied, flipping a couple of pages in my math book.

I shrugged. "I don't know that you'd be much help. Unless you can make logarithms make sense, which no math teacher has ever been able to do, then I think I'm screwed."

Kelsey wrinkled her nose. "Nope, sorry. I understand how they work, but I don't think I could explain it if I tried."

I sighed. "Have I mentioned that I hate math?" I asked. She nodded with a smile. "Hey, where's your distraction?" I prodded. "I need one."

Her smile grew. "So," she said excitedly, "I have found the perfect guy to set you up with. You'll really like him." I set down my pencil.

"I'm listening."

"He's super nice. He's got a great smile, he's taller than you, he's just a great guy." She was selling him pretty hard.

"Sounds good to me," I replied. "As long as there's no 'but' to everything that you just said."

She laughed and shook her head. "Okay, so he wants me to figure out when you guys can go out. He was hoping you'd be free next weekend." I opened up the calendar on my phone.

"Next weekend? Really? That's Valentine's Day." I grimaced. "Doesn't that put like a lot of extra pressure on both of us?"

Kelsey leaned over to look at the phone. "Valentine's Day is on Sunday. You could go on Friday or Saturday night. That's not Valentine's Day," she pointed out matter-of-factly. I made a face at her.

"Semantics," I muttered. "Can't we wait? Or just go tomorrow?"

She shook her head. "His work schedule is really tricky. He works most nights and rarely has weekends off. Next weekend is the only time for the next month that he can go."

"I can't imagine why he would want to spend his only night off in a month on a blind date," I mused. Kelsey smiled.

"He really wants to meet you," she reassured. "He knows all about you by now, and he's really excited."

I sighed in surrender. "Friday it is, then. The farther away from Sunday the better. Should I call him?"

Kelsey shook her head quickly. "No, I'll talk to him."

I shrugged. "Whatever," I looked at her hopefully. "Any more distractions?"

She shook her head sadly. "Nope, sorry," she lamented, sliding off my bed. "I wish I did. I have to go write a paper."

"Good luck," I called after her, wishing I could write a paper instead and turned back to the open books on my bed.

The week flew by in a blur of papers, assignments, and tests. Thursday rolled around and I realized that I had never gotten any details from Kelsey about the mystery man. She worked late on campus Thursday nights, so I sat in the common room reading until she came in.

"Hey," she said, closing the door behind her. Her bookstore uniform was a blinding orange polo.

"Hey," I replied, shielding my eyes from the gaudy color. "So, you never told me, did you ever set up a date with that guy?"

She pulled the refrigerator opened and stuck her head in. "Mmphhoonsmetpphth," came the muffled response. I hopped off the couch and pulled the fridge open wider.

"Maybe try that again," I advised, watching her pop another couple of grapes into her mouth. She held up a finger while she chewed.

"Yes," she said after finally swallowing. "Tomorrow night. He will meet you at Willow Creek Grill at 7:00." She popped another couple of grapes in her mouth.

"Do I get a name? Description? Anything?" I prodded. She nodded, and once again, had to finish chewing.

"He's tall. Dark hair. His name is JT. He said he'll wear a blue shirt. He's seen your picture, so you can wear whatever you want," she added with a smile.

"Sounds good," I replied, stealing a grape from her. "That means I can raid your closet!" I laughed and disappeared into her room, Kelsey following close behind.

I ended up in Kelsey's turquoise lace top, skinny jeans, and tall black boots. Kelsey insisted that I curl my hair, and even let me borrow her favorite sequined cardigan. I gave myself a once over in the full-length mirror and smiled my approval. I loved having a roommate with good taste. Willow Creek wasn't too far to walk, but considering the heels on the boots, that was out of the question.

"I'll drop you off," Kelsey offered. "JT can give you a ride home."

I looked at her with eyebrows raised. "I know that you approve, Kels, but what if he's a creeper? I don't want him to know where I live. Can't I just borrow your car?"

She sighed and shook her head. "I need it tonight. If he freaks you out, just text me and I'll come get you." I didn't love it, but I didn't have much of a choice, either.

We pulled up in front of the crowded restaurant. I waved goodbye and hopped out of the car.

"Have fun!" she called as she pulled away from the curb. I had never been to Willow Creek before, but it definitely smelled good. I pulled out my phone to check the time. I was a couple of minutes early, but I headed inside, hoping to find a place to sit. The boots may have been chic, but they were not super comfortable. I found a single empty chair in the front lobby and claimed it, hoping that JT would show up soon so that I didn't have to feel guilty the next time someone who deserved the chair more than I did showed up. I gazed at the walls, studying the generic artwork, and when that didn't hold my attention, I began to people watch. I was just studying a couple, obviously fellow college students, and wondering which date they were on, when the door opened and a rush of cold air blew past me for the umpteenth time. I glanced over to see if it was JT, and my jaw dropped. Tall, dark hair, and in a blue shirt. James. Kelsey was so dead.

chapter thirty-five

February 2018

James hadn't noticed me yet, and I took advantage. He looked nervous, his hands in his pockets, his jaw clenched. I stayed where I was, staring, until his eyes landed on me. A small, apologetic smile appeared as he approached.

"Sydney," he said. I kept my face passive.

"James," I responded, my tone reflecting my expression. "What brings you to Boise?" I asked sardonically. My question threw him off guard.

"I came to see you," he said slowly.

"Oh, I'm sorry," I replied. "I'm meeting someone here."

His jaw tightened momentarily until he realized I was messing with him. "Syd," he said pleadingly. I kept my face as expressionless as ever. "I've got a reservation," he explained. "Just let me buy you dinner. If you never want to see me again by the end of the night, I'll leave and I won't come back."

I stood reluctantly and followed him to the hostess station. We were seated quickly and I kept my eyes on the menu and off of James.

"How have you been?" he asked hesitantly. I shrugged noncommittally.

"Fine," I responded without looking. I wondered how guilty I would feel after dinner if I milked him for all he was worth and got the most expensive thing on the menu.

"I didn't want to let things just end so unresolved," he began.

"Mmmhmm," I murmured. I could go with the Petit Filet, but the Mahi Mahi looked even better.

"I wanted to apologize, and I was hoping for a chance to maybe, go back to the way things were." I heard his nerves as his voice wavered slightly.

I could feel his eyes on me, but I kept mine resolutely on the menu. "Right," I said. Maybe I would go for an appetizer too. Oooh, crab cakes.

"Sydney!" James snatched my menu out of my hands. "I drove all the way up here to see you. The least you can do is listen to me!"

I cocked my head deliberately to the side and narrowed my eyes at him. "I'm sorry," I began slowly, the words drenched with sarcasm. "I'm. So. Sorry," I repeated, punctuating each syllable. "You drove all the way up here? That must have been a real sacrifice for you, James. Should I be flattered? Should I be flattered after you tell me that you never want to see me again, and you just show up? Or should I be flattered that you somehow conned my roommate into setting this all up for you?" With each question my voice got louder and louder. "Or should I be flattered that you *swore* to Gavin that nothing would ever happen between us?" His eyes were wide. "I don't know what you were expecting, James. You make no effort to so much as talk to me for three months, and all of a sudden you show up, expecting me to what, fall at your feet?" I glared at him and he glared right back, speechless. I noticed a waitress approach, but she caught wind of the showdown and wisely backed away.

"Really, Sydney? You think you're the only one that has had a crappy couple of months? Not only did I screw things up with my best friend, I also blew my shot with the girl I love. I have never been more miserable in my entire life. So get off your soap box and listen to me for a minute!"

I sat back in my chair in surprise, the menu forgotten on the table. "Love?" I asked softly.

"What?" he snapped, not expecting this turn in the argument.

"You said the girl you love. You love me?" My voice had dropped to barely above a whisper.

James looked flustered. He raked his fingers through his hair nervously and then studied me for a few moments, a strange look of determination on his face.

"I love you," he began resignedly. "I love your smile and your eyes and the way that you don't finish your sentences when you ask me a question and the way you get all grumpy when you are doing math and the way that your nose scrunches up when you're frustrated and the way you get really cold all the time and the way that you tell me everything in your life and the way that you always quote *The Princess Bride* and the way you sing the songs that I hate really loud and the way you look right now and the way you make me crazy." He sat back in his chair, his eyes lingering on my face. I stared back at him, speechless. The waitress chose that moment to reapproach.

"Welcome to Willow Creek Grill. Can I get you some drinks to get you started?" she asked, glancing back and forth between the two of us. I looked at her blankly.

"Two waters. With lemon. And we're going to need a few minutes," James said, shifting his gaze to her. She nodded briefly and was gone again. He turned back to me, waiting for a response.

"You love me," I said again in a daze. James laughed shortly.

"I think that's been pretty well established," he commented, picking his menu back up. We were quiet until our water arrived. My mind raced. He loves me. It wasn't just some stupid crush. He loves me. He came up here to tell me. He loves me. I am going to kill Kelsey. He loves me. Did she call him or did he call her? He loves me. Probably no crab cakes now. He loves me.

"I don't know what to say," I said slowly. James sighed.

"Well, this wasn't exactly how I planned for this conversation to go, so I'm not really sure what to say either." He rubbed the back of his neck nervously. I looked at him curiously.

"How did you plan for it to go?" I asked, running my fingertips along the edge of the menu.

"You want me to start over?"

I shrugged. "Might as well."

James nodded slowly. "Okay," he replied skeptically. "I was going to apologize for the way everything happened. I was going to apologize for the way Gavin found out." He winced as he spoke. "I was going to apologize for the way I treated you at the cabin. I was going to tell you how much I missed you. I was going to ask if you thought we could try to be friends again." He paused and looked at me hopefully.

"But you weren't going to tell me you loved me?" I asked.

He grinned sheepishly. "I thought about maybe working up to that," he said. "But only if things went really, really well."

"James," I began hesitantly, pushing my hair behind one ear and leaning forward, "why did you come?"

His brow furrowed. "I just told you," he replied, confused. I shook my head.

"Why are you here now? Why didn't you come see me over the break? I've been up here for six weeks. Why are you here now?"

"I knew that Gavin came to see you. New Year's Eve. I couldn't interfere again. If that's what you wanted, to be with him, if that's what would make you happy, then it didn't really matter what I wanted."

"Oh," I replied faintly, processing what he had just said.

"But I didn't know that you turned him down. I didn't know until a couple of weeks ago and I thought about letting you go, but I couldn't. I didn't think you'd talk to me, so I tracked down your roommate."

The waitress came back and we ordered. Dinner was fantastic, and we talked all the way through it, almost like nothing had ever happened. When the waitress began to clear the table, I realized that the night was almost over. And I didn't know where to go from here.

"So, now what?" I asked as James took a sip of his water. He furrowed his brow and set his glass down.

"We can get dessert, if you want," he replied, misunderstanding the question. I shook my head quickly.

"No, I mean, you want us to be friends, but you love me, but you live in Utah and I live in Boise. Just, well, now what?" I repeated, searching his face for an answer. He narrowed his eyes at me.

"I don't know what to do, Sydney. What do you want to do?"

"We are not going to play the 'I don't know, what do you want to do' game with our lives, James," I replied, all of a sudden annoyed.

"I'll transfer to Boise, I'll apply to Cal Arts. We'll figure it out." He reached out for my hand.

I shook my head. "It's not that simple."

"Why not?"

"I don't even know where I'll be next year, James. I don't know if I can afford to stay up here and I definitely can't afford California. I can't ask you to put your life, your education on hold while you wait for me to figure out mine."

"You're not asking me to," he replied.

"I mean it, James. I won't let you give up what you want for me," I was insistent.

"Sydney," he said slowly. "You're what I want."

I took a deep breath. "And I can't do long distance again. I'm not sure if I can handle being hours and hours away from the man I love. It's hard, James, and it hurts." I stopped talking at the look on his face. "What?"

"You said 'the man you love,'" he pointed out.

"What?"

"You love me?" he asked, a smile playing around the corners of his mouth. I bit my lip, realizing what I had just said. I looked up at him and studied his face, my eyes locked on his.

"I love you," I said with a hint of surprise. The smile on his face grew.

"C'mon," he said, getting to his feet. "Let's go." He slid some cash into the check and pulled me out of my chair. We walked slowly to his car, hand in hand. As we arrived, he turned to face me. "I love you too," he said, leaning close to me. He wrapped an arm around my waist. I began to melt into him, but stopped with a jolt, realizing that nothing had been decided.

"Wait!" I said sharply. He pulled back a bit, but didn't move his arm. "We didn't figure anything out. We still don't know what we're going to do!" Rather than release me, he tightened his grip and pulled me closer.

"I know exactly what we're going to do," he said softly, resting his forehead against mine. "I love you, Sydney Morris, and I plan on doing whatever is necessary to be with you."

I smiled up at him. "Okay," I said. And then his lips covered mine and stayed there until my phone began to ring. I pulled back, reaching for it. His hand closed over mine.

"It's Kelsey," I protested. "She probably wants to know what happened." A smile parted James's lips.

"She can wait," he said gently, pulling me closer.

I leaned my head against his chest and murmured quietly, "As you wish."

discussion questions

1. How has Sydney's parent's divorce affected the way she values relationships?

2. Sydney takes very seriously her role as her mother's help and support. How does that affect the way that she relates to Gavin and to James?

3. Do you think that Sydney's level of guilt is justified?

4. What are some ways that you relate to Sydney or James?

about the author

Lindsay Walden Photography

Rachel grew up reading every book she could get her hands on and spending time with her cat. At least, that was the report in every annual Christmas letter. The humiliation was enough to spur her into action, and she began writing, and never stopped. Rachel studied English at Brigham Young University—Idaho and then blogged and wrote in between the births of her six children. She currently lives in West Jordan with her family, and while she no longer has a cat, she still reads every book she can get her hands on. *Right Next to Me* is her second novel.

Scan to visit

screamandhug.blogspot.com